The Silent Connection

By

Pauline K Murfin

Joanna always knew her daughter Holly was special. The fact that she was profoundly deaf never altered her giving and gentle nature.

So when Holly met William, who had been locked away inside his own world for three years (since his apparent stroke). Their connection was instant. William was cared for by his adoring wife Lilly who could see only too well the effect Holly had on him.

If the only way to give their children the best possible advantage was to move to the Royal School for the deaf in Derbyshire, then Joanna (and her new found friends Joel Alisha and their daughter Precious) would move – even if their finances would force them to house share.

They had given everything for the needs of their children, but it was time to rejoin the outside world. They couldn't protect their children from the inevitable when all they wanted was to experience it.

When Lilly and William needed help and Joanna and Holly were able to give it, who would know that all of their lives would change? Especially when Joanna met Simon their son – the handsome airline pilot who would be instrumental in changing all of their futures.

Pauline Murfin is a sixty one year old mother, with three grown up sons.

Married for forty two years to husband Graham, they live in a remote village in Northumberland. Pauline and her husband Graham moved to a small village which is part of the Kielder Forest in the Northumberland National Park in 1999. Poor health prevented Pauline from working, so she decided to study for a degree with The Open University. "To keep my brain ticking over", after completing her degree and gaining a Bachelor of Science she turns her hand to writing fiction.

"Something I have always wanted to do" says Pauline.

Also by Pauline K Murfin

To Begin Again

Comraich

Dreams Lost Dreams Found

This book is dedicated to my friends and family.
Without whose help it would not have been possible.

To my dear friends Blanche and Elizabeth, thank you
once again. My two wonderful proof readers – who get
to have a good laugh at my expense, while correcting,
my spelling and grammar errors.

To Blanche, whose opinion I can always count on being
the truth.
To Elizabeth, who has never worked so hard since she
retired.

And to Pat Potts, for believing in me.

To Graham my technical support team. Without his help
I would not even be able to repair the printer.

To my copy editor, Lori Heaford. Thank you Lori, once
again for your sympathetic interpretation of my raw
manuscript.

And finally, thank you to Val McMahon, who inspired
me to write my fourth novel. I will always be grateful as
I had forgotten how enjoyable I find writing.

Chapter 1

Sitting in the passenger seat of the little red post van, Holly waited patiently for her mummy to come back from delivering the post to the people in the old station house. She loved being with her mum during the school holidays. Although she loved her school too, Holly liked to meet all different types of people, not just those who are deaf.

As she sat watching out of the window, her eye was attracted to a group of workmen climbing up and down a ladder leaning against the house. As she had nothing better to do, she found herself automatically looking at their lips to read what they were saying. It's a bit like eavesdropping on a conversation you accidentally overhear: it's not something you set out to do but you listen all the same.

Holly wasn't sure if she had understood the men correctly. They seemed to be saying that they intended to 'rip off the tiles because there was going to be a big storm that night', but surely, Holly thought, that couldn't be right?

Intrigued now, she looked more closely. The tallest of the three men seemed to be telling the other two scruffy-looking ones to take off enough tiles to make the roof leak. Then put a tarp on.

What is a tarp? wondered Holly. The smaller of the scruffy men went to a flatbed truck parked in the large yard of the old station, which now served as a drive, and brought out a large blue sheet.

Ahh, thought Holly, a tarp is a waterproof sheet.

She continued to watch the conversation between one of the small scruffy men and the tall one who seemed to be the boss; well, he was the one that did all the talking anyway. He was telling them to put the tarp on the roof but not to fix it down, as it's going to be nice and windy tonight, and they all laughed.

Holly was sure she had missed something in translation because what would be funny about the house letting in the rain and wouldn't the 'tarp' blow away if it's going to be really windy?

When Holly's mum climbed back into the van calling "Cheerio" over her shoulder, Holly was still trying to understand the conversation she had unwittingly eavesdropped on. Joanna turned to Holly with a smile, asking, "Are you okay?"

"Mmm," said Holly still looking puzzled, "Mummy, why would it be funny if rain leaked into the lady's house?"

"What do you mean, Holly? Leaked into whose house?"

Holly relayed the story as she saw it, still very perplexed as to why it would be funny if the wind got so bad that the tarp blew away.

Joanna looked at Holly closely, and asked, "Are you sure, Holly? Are you sure that's what they were saying?"

"Oh yes, Mummy, the tall man told one of the scruffy men to rip enough tiles off the roof so the rain would leak in. And he told the other scruffy man to put on the tarp, but not to fix it because it was going to be nice and windy tonight and they all laughed.

"Why would they want the rain to get into the house? Won't the people inside get wet?"

Joanna was a bit stunned and asked Holly if she was absolutely positive that's what they had said, although she knew that Holly was not prone to fantasy. She was also an excellent lip reader, as she had learned from being a toddler. So there was absolutely no way she would make a mistake.

Joanna carried on with her round but became more and more agitated and convinced that something untoward was going on at the old station. She decided the minute she finished her deliveries she would go back and at least tell the old couple what Holly had overheard.

Oh, that should be good, thought Joanna; trying to tell an elderly couple that my eight-year-old daughter, who is deaf, overheard their builders plotting to rip them off and no doubt charge them for some rather expensive repair job.

However, she knew her conscience would not allow her to ignore what Holly had seen. She also knew Holly would not let it drop until she had an answer. She'd always been the same ever since she was a small child; which was probably how she managed her deafness. It was as though the world was deaf and she was no different from anyone else.

She was the most beautiful child, as though she had been given extra beauty to make up for the lack of hearing. Holly was not simply beauty on the outside; she had the most loving nature, too. If ever there had been a moment of doubt as to whether Joanna regretted having a baby who had changed the course of her life, the moment was short-lived. Joanna knew her life had been the richer because of Holly, just as she knew that Holly's father Kevin would have loved Holly as much as she did, had he lived.

Holly didn't take after Kevin for her looks. In fact, although there were very few photographs of Joanna when she was Holly's age, she knew that they could have been twins. Joanna's naturally wavy, thick blonde hair framed her face, and her healthy tan, acquired by being a postwoman, made her blue eyes all the more noticeable. There was what the Victorians would have called a 'countenance' about Joanna. She was always happy and smiling – it was as though from an early age she had decided she would be happy and make the best of life – and it showed. Her job as a postwoman had served her well and she loved it. Even though she had her newly acquired degree and could probably do much better for herself, she wasn't in any hurry to move on.

The wind was becoming stronger, coming in gusts now, and the rain was so heavy the windscreen wipers were going as fast as they could yet the screen was still permanently blurred as they turned back towards the old station.

Deciding it would not be a good idea to leave Holly in the van this time, Joanna parked the van and they made a run for the house. Joanna knocked heavily at the front door, knowing all the time it would take Mrs Winter a while to answer it as she had her ankle plaster to drag with her following her fiasco with the ladder.

All the time they cowered in the doorway as the rain lashed and the wind gathered speed, Joanna wondered if this was a terrible mistake. How on earth was she going to convince this lady of their suspicions without sounding like something from *Murder, She Wrote*?

Just then a voice from behind the door shouted, "I'm coming! Sorry it's taking me so long, I'll be there in a minute."

Just then the very old, heavy black door opened and a light shone through from the hall. Mrs Winter was a tall, slim lady in her late sixties, although still very smart. However, at present she was slightly bent over and leaning on a stick, which she was using for support while she had this rather chunky white plaster on her ankle and foot. Peering out of the door into the fast disappearing light of the late afternoon, she was totally surprised to see her post lady and a child.

"Hello, Mrs Winter, I'm sorry to bother you, but I would like to have a word with you, if that's all right?"

Mrs Winter smiled, a little puzzled. However, good manners required her to ask Joanna and the little girl into the warmth of the house and away from the howling wind.

"Come in, my dear, gosh the weather's dreadful, isn't it? I hope it doesn't get any worse until my builders can return to mend my roof."

By this time they had reached the living room. Joanna saw whom she presumed to be Mr Winter, in the corner of the warm, homely sitting room; he was sat in a large leather armchair, next to a roaring fire. A blank expression on his elderly face, (older than Mrs Winter by maybe ten years, Joanna thought), the only outward sign that he was aware they had entered the room or that something was different was his constant clasping and unclasping of his fingers on the knees of his trousers.

"This is William, my husband. He doesn't like the wind and to make matters worse the tarpaulin the builders have put on is making a terrible noise and it confuses and frightens him. Anyway, I'm terribly sorry, I'm wittering on about wind and tarpaulins and you have come about something far more important, I'm sure."

"Well, to be honest, Mrs Winter—"

"Lily, please call us Lily and William."

"Your builders are exactly what I have come to talk to you about! Look, I don't know how to say this, but my daughter Holly, who is deaf, overheard your builders. Well, I say overheard but that's not what I mean."

Trying not to become flustered so as not to complicate things, Joanna started again. "You see, Mrs...erm...Lily, Holly is deaf but she lip reads perfectly, and—"

Joanna abruptly paused in attempting to explain to Mrs Winter what Holly had seen, and both women turned towards Holly, who, totally out of character, was stretching her hand out in the direction of Mr Winter's agitated fingers, which were writhing back and forth on his trousers. The strangest thing happened then. Mr Winter seemed to be drawn to look at Holly, and she to him. He saw her outstretched fingers and, to Mrs Winter's absolute amazement, he stretched one of his own hands tentatively towards them.

As their fingers touched it was as though a light switched on inside the empty eyes and his gentle face appeared to have life once more. Holly gave him one of her beautiful smiles, her cornflower blue eyes sparkling. Her smile must have been contagious, as his thin lips turned up at the corners. Holly signed and spoke simultaneously as she always did for those who didn't understand 'sign'.

"My name is Holly, what's yours?"

After what seemed an age William looked to Lily for confirmation.

"William, your name is William," Lily reassured him. Then, turning to Joanna, she said, "Well, I'll go to the foot of our stairs; I haven't seen William show any interest in the outside world for a long, long time." Then, to Holly, "Oh, my dear, you are a wonder child. Deaf, you say? Well, that must be why you are special and oh so pretty. William must like you, my dear."

Mrs Winter mouthed very obviously so that Holly could see what she was saying. Phew, thought Joanna. At least she wasn't going to have to try explaining what seemed impossible to most hearing people: that someone can understand perfectly by lip reading and that the fact they are deaf does not mean they are stupid.

Joanna attempted again to explain why they had come back. After she had conveyed what Holly had seen, and her fear that the builders had deliberately sabotaged the roof tiles in order to come back and charge money for work that probably didn't really need doing, Mrs Winter said, "Oh no, I'm sure you're mistaken, dear, because the 'boss' person got one of his men to put a tarpaulin over to make sure that we don't have any water getting in. He is so busy at the moment, but, when he came back, he said it's a good job he looked because there are many more jobs to do. He said the chimney stack is dangerous and also something about 'flashing'? Erm…not sure but, anyway, with the weather on the turn and winter coming; and I don't want to bother Simon, my son, with trivialities. He's a pilot, you know," offered Lily proudly, "and he has a very stressful job and I don't like to pester him with household worries."

"But Lily, I'm afraid you are being ripped off. Holly definitely saw them discussing tearing more tiles off so the roof would definitely leak. That is supposed to convince you to have the roof mended. Then they tell you lots more jobs need doing; it's a scam! They will ask for money next; and usually the price goes up as soon as they actually get on the roof and find more supposed jobs that need doing."

"Oh well, actually they have asked for money, but only enough for the materials and labour, he said," Lily answered.

"How much have they asked for, if you don't mind me asking? I know it seems forward of me; it's just that I've heard of these scams before and don't want you to get ripped off."

"Well, they have asked for two thousand up front."

Joanna gulped in shock at the sheer amount.

Lily went on, "And, presumably, the residue later, but I'm sure you're wrong, dear. There was a loose slate, that's how I broke my ankle. I thought I could do the job myself without bothering Simon with it. He gets home so little and, when he does, I don't like to ask him to be working on the house, even though it's his home. We just live in what used to be the ticket office, which is large enough and manageable for William and me. I got the ladder and I could see the slate just wanted pushing in so I did it. Everything was fine until I lost my balance and fell, silly me. Simon was furious when I had to tell him over the phone. I wouldn't have told him but he would have soon found out when he saw my plaster."

"Oh, Lily, please don't give them any money. Leave it until your son comes home; honestly, I know in my bones this is a scam. Holly is never mistaken. They even said that they were going to leave the tarpaulin loose so that it would flap in the wind, which is designed to make you even more afraid and more likely to let them go ahead with as many so-called 'little jobs' as they can get away with. When are you supposed to pay them the money?"

"Well, I was going to get a taxi to the bank tomorrow. I don't like leaving William, but he is usually fine if I put the television on for him. He may not even notice for the length of time I would be away."

"Please don't draw any money yet. Would you let me have a look tomorrow in the daylight? You say they are not coming back for a few days? Well, that would be right because they want you to worry, so in the end you will agree to anything. Will you let me have a look? If I can see real damage then it's up to you, but if I can only see a few tiles that they have ripped off will you believe me and tell them you have decided to wait until your son comes home?"

"Well... I suppose it can't do any harm. After all, they won't be coming for a day or two. I'm sure you're wrong, but I'm not silly. If Holly said she saw them and she has no reason not to tell the truth, then it would be irresponsible of me not to listen. But oh, my dear, I couldn't let you go climbing on the roof – look what happened to me! No, no, I couldn't."

"I won't be climbing on any roof; I will only need to peep under the cover. That should tell us what we need to know. So that's agreed. I will be here first thing in the morning, okay?"

Joanna turned to indicate to Holly that it was time to go. She smiled to herself when she saw her sitting quite innocently holding William's hand, which had had the most amazing affect on him and his apparent agitation. He was totally calm now, and they were both sat watching the flickering flames in the open fire.

Holly stood up and gave William's hand a little squeeze, saying and signing, "Bye, bye, William."

Lily saw them out into the evening light and gathering storm, saying she would see them tomorrow. She gave Holly's shoulder a squeeze, and as the girl turned back she mouthed the words, 'Bye, bye, Holly'.

Chapter 2

The short drive home told Joanna that the rain and the wind were only just starting. She would be surprised if the tarpaulin wasn't halfway into town by the morning.

She pulled into the drive of the comfortable four-bedroom house she and Holly shared with Joel, Alisha and their little girl Precious, a West Indian family. It was an arrangement they had set up many years ago that had seemed like an enormous risk at the time, to house share with people you had only just met, simply because their little girl was also deaf and was to attend the same day nursery as Holly, but it suited them both.

Joanna had asked for a transfer from the Post Office where she worked, to allow her to do her Open Uni degree in her spare time. It meant moving to a strange area, a different city. She hadn't even been to Derby until she was trying to find a school for the deaf who took children in from as young as three. Her previous employer had provided day care for Holly so that Joanna could work more or less full-time, to pay her own way.

It wasn't only difficult for her and Holly; it was equally bad for Joel and Alisha. Joel was in his final year of training to become a doctor and Alisha was just completing her exams to become a qualified nurse. They later found out they had all had a really difficult three years, trying to cope, not only with jobs and careers, but also with babies they were to find were profoundly deaf.

Staying at the same B & B overnight while checking out nursery schools turned out to be a godsend for Joanna, Joel and Alisha. Who would then have thought that in five years they would still be happily house sharing? In fact they didn't really think of it that way now; it was as though they were one big family.

Joanna and Holly dashed into the house out of the horrendous weather shouting that they were home. As usual, if Alisha was home first, the most wonderful appetising smell would emanate from the kitchen. Joanna hadn't realised how hungry she was until the smell reached her nostrils and she rubbed her hands together to indicate to Holly that she couldn't wait for her supper. Holly did the same.

"I love it when Alisha cooks, Mummy; not that you can't cook, but her food is lush."

They hurried into the large family kitchen, which they actually spent most of their time in as it was so people friendly with a comfy sofa and a log burner. Alisha was standing over the stove like a magician stirring what seemed to be a dozen cooking pots and pans.

"Hello, you two, how was your day? Dinner won't be long. Joel won't be in until later as he has drawn the short straw at the hospital." Then, "Precious is upstairs," Alisha signed to Holly.

She continued, "You're late, aren't you? The rain, I suppose, dreadful. It's going to be a terrible night tonight; I'm glad I'm on days this week and not nights."

"Wow, look at the time, I hadn't realised," Joanna replied. "Yes, we came across a bit of a problem."

As Holly had disappeared upstairs it was left to Joanna to explain about the roofers, saying that she was positive they had targeted the elderly couple because Mr Winter seemed to have dementia or something. Mrs Winter, Lily, she commented was as bright as a button, but described how she had broken her ankle climbing up a ladder to fix a loose roof tile.

"So you don't think it's possible the roof actually does need retiling?" Alisha asked.

"No, I'm positive what Holly saw was them discussing a scam to rip the old couple off; and I'm going to make sure they don't get away with it."

"Ha, well now you have finished your degree you can put it to good use. I always knew you would be a 'people's advocate'. Law and social care, what better combination for a bleeding heart radical?"

"Ha, look who's talking, Florence Nightingale! How long after your shift has finished do you actually leave the hospital, hmmm?" Joanna countered.

"Well, that's different. You can't just walk out in the middle of a dressing, or from getting a bed pan for someone, now, can you?"

"Let's face it: between you, me and Joel, we carry the world's conscience on our shoulders. We're all guilty but it makes us 'finer human beings', I say, ha ha."

Changing the subject, Alisha told her, "Give the girls a call, will you? Supper's ready. I'll set a place for Joel in case he makes it home in time."

Joanna went to the bottom of the stairs and flicked the passage light on and off to let the girls know they were wanted. As she sat down at the table, both she and Alisha rolled their eyes at what sounded like a herd of elephants bounding down the stairs as though they were coming through the ceiling.

It was a complete myth that there was a lot of silence where deaf people were concerned. In fact, it was just the opposite; nobody would believe how noisy deaf children can be. Holly and Precious had no idea how loudly they spoke or laughed or giggled, which they frequently did, as all young girls do. Did all girls squeal? Joanna often wondered. She could never remember doing that as a child, although she had never had the privilege of feeling the security of a home life, where she wasn't constantly on her best behaviour in case she was moved on for whatever reason.

Having been fostered most of her life, Joanna had had to grow up very quickly. She had learned from an early age to be well behaved, quiet and unobtrusive, giving no reason for a foster family to get rid of her. However, no matter how much she tried to stay in the background, she was always moved on to yet another well-meaning family.

They had just sat down to supper when they heard Joel come into the passage complaining about the terrible weather, how his car wouldn't start, how he thought it was going to need a new battery for the winter, and oh, isn't it a horrible night? "I hate the winter," he grumbled on, talking to nobody in particular, by which time he'd arrived in the kitchen.

Walking through the door, he saw the wry expressions on Alisha's and Joanna's faces. He knew, of course, what their faces were saying. They'd told him many times before that his conversation started in the passage and if there happened to be nobody in the kitchen it would mean he was talking to himself.

He ignored their smug expressions and went through the rest of his usual routine: with one finger pointing to each cheek he would say "Plant it there" and the girls would giggle and kiss him. "Am I not the master in my own house?" he would say, at which everyone would fall about laughing as Joel simply wasn't capable of being the master of anything. He was the original gentle giant. He was totally useless at DIY, too: in fact, it was a household joke that if you wanted anything doing you should ask Joanna. With the wind howling outside Joanna could not stop thinking about poor Mr and Mrs Winter. God, she hoped their tarpaulin kept the rain out until tomorrow morning – at least until she could assess the damage.

"You don't mean to tell me you are going to climb on the roof and check for damage?" Joel was incredulous, after Joanna and Holly had relayed the story once again about the roofing villains, as Holly called them.

Joanna nodded, asking what else could she do?

"I've got to be at the hospital early in the morning – my clinic starts at nine – but I could—"

"Ha ha, no thank you, Joel. You are very kind, but to be honest I think I will manage better on my own."

Alisha joined in, telling Joel that if it didn't stop him seeing stars or keep the rain off him, he wouldn't know which side of the house was up.

"Now I object to that," Joel protested. "I'm sure I would know, and actually I was only going to offer to hold the ladder while Joanna climbed up, but I would have been up there in spirit, giving her support."

Everyone laughed. Even the girls saw the funny side of Joel helping anyone do an outside job. As the girls retreated upstairs, Alisha and Joel snuggled up on the sofa, their banter an obvious sign of their continuing affection for each other.

In an exaggerated Caribbean accent, Joel joked, "When they ask me at the hospital, 'Hey, Joel, what's it like living with four women? I tell them, hey man, it's like having my own harem. I am the man of that house.' I don't know why they laugh; I am the boss man in this house." Alisha almost choked on her coffee.

Joanna laughed from the kitchen sink, where she was washing the dishes. There was an unwritten agreement that whoever cooked did not do the washing up, and whoever did the washing never did the ironing, on the whole anyway, unless it was Joel's turn to cook. He loved to be in the kitchen cooking and he didn't mind cleaning up either. However, those were rare occasions when he was not working long, hard hours at the hospital.

Chapter 3

The following morning was a typical October day. However, the worst of the storm seemed to have blown itself out and the rain had ceased for the time being, although the sky churned with dark clouds and chinks of sun filtered through now and again. Actually, Joanna liked this type of morning, as soon as it became light, bearing in mind that she was up at five and it was rarely light then unless it was the height of summer.

But on mornings like this she could smell the autumn, she would say. The air was fresh, and not muggy, as it was in the summer. No, on the whole, this was Joanna's favourite season. She was just glad today that the weather had held so she could climb the ladder at the Winters' place.

She had promised to double back and collect Holly before she went to call on Mr and Mrs Winter. She knew how Holly loved meeting people, especially elderly people, her deafness in no way putting her off. Joanna thought it was probably because she didn't see her grandparents very often.

Kevin's birth parents were both profoundly deaf, which was the reason he had been put up for adoption (something Kevin never knew). It was frowned upon that a couple who were not particularly young and were labelled 'disabled' had a baby. It was assumed they would not know how to look after a child.

One cannot imagine that ever happening now. However, it is not so long ago when social services ruled, and presided over all those who were unable to speak for themselves. When Joanna and Kevin met, on the same course at university, their intentions were to change the world, especially the adoption and fostering system; sadly neither of them was to achieve their goal.

It was by pure chance that Joanna had found the address that Kevin had waited so impatiently for. Having nobody that cared enough to collect his few things from their halls of residence after the accident, Joanna had taken it upon herself to take his little bits and pieces – nothing of any value, mostly records, posters and a shoebox full of childhood memories that he treasured. There were a few bits of mail, too, which was where

Joanna would find the address unopened later, while looking through his belongings after the birth of their baby.

Joanna had vowed to take her and Kevin's baby to visit them so that his parents could know that he had never given up looking for them. Nothing could have prepared Joanna for the shock of finding out that not only were Kevin's parents much older than she had expected but also that they were both profoundly deaf.

This answered so many questions for Joanna. There had been no possible way to trace her own past as her birth mother had been a junkie and an alcoholic, or so she had been told by the social worker. So there were no medical or social history records and no way of knowing if the deafness was from her genes or Kevin's.

Joanna never forgot that his parents, knowing and understanding that she was a single parent and would need help, had offered any assistance they could; but it had been obvious from the outset that, although their hearts were in the right place, they were unable to do anything for her. They did offer her a room if she needed somewhere to stay and they bought little baby clothes and sent them by post, often with a ten-pound note pushed inside.

Joanna did try to keep in touch but the visits became fewer and fewer as Joanna had to leave her university course unfinished to find work. She would never forget how lucky she was to find her job at the Royal Mail, who had offered her flexible hours and the use of the baby crèche. Although she had barely made ends meet, living in her bedsit, she had vowed that she would never, ever let history repeat itself and put her child up for fostering or adoption. She had promised herself, too, that she would complete her course, even if it meant studying during the night, which invariably it did. And at last, a little later than she had originally planned when she was eighteen and at university, she completed her course in law and social care.

Arriving at the old station, Joanna found no sign of the blue tarpaulin that had been flapping in the wind the night before. Not at all surprised by this, Joanna pulled into the old station yard drive and there lay the tarpaulin covered in dead leaves and rain water.

"Oh, poor William and Lily, I hope they are all right," she said.

Holly could hardly wait for the engine to stop before jumping out of the van to run to the front door. It opened almost immediately, as though Lily had been watching for their arrival.

"Oh, my dear, I don't know what to do," Lily fretted. "The boss of the outfit rang this morning and said that he has fitted me in for tomorrow as he knows how desperate we are, but he will need the money up front for materials. I didn't know what to say so I just said all right. Is that all right?"

"Right, don't panic," advised Joanna. "I will go straight away and have a little look. Then I will decide what to do. If you could just hold the ladder, that's all you have to do. Holly will stay with William, all right?"

Holly was sitting with William as though they had known each other forever.

As Joanna had suspected, the only tiles that the men had been bothered to remove were those closest to the edge, and even then they numbered only half a dozen tiles. She looked towards the chimney stack, which actually looked newly pointed in Joanna's limited experience. It certainly did not need anything done to it, least of all the 'flashing' the roofers had said needed doing, which referred to a sort of lead bandage that covers joins. No, the Winters' roof and chimney all looked fine and waterproof to Joanna.

As she climbed down the ladder, Joanna noted that Lily was hanging on to it for dear life, though whether it was as a crutch to hold herself up or to steady Joanna as she precariously clambered down each rung, Joanna couldn't tell. At least they didn't end up in a heap.

"Well, well what do you think? What did it look like to you?" Lily asked.

"Well, Lily," Joanna told her, "it's just as I suspected: there is no major work to be done, the chimney stack looks to be freshly pointed and the flashing looks perfect to me. The only tiles I can see missing are the ones right on the edge, which we could actually push back in. In fact, that's them leaning against the wall and most of them look intact. I suspect they were even going to use your own tiles. Two thousand for materials indeed! Let's go inside and we will think up our game plan."

Sitting down with a coffee, Lily seemed less agitated.

Joanna laid out her plan: "All you have to say when they ring is that you have been in touch with your son and he is going to do the jobs himself. Then you thank him very much for his trouble and tell him, if he puts a bill in for putting the tarpaulin up, your son will pay it as soon as he gets home."

"And do you think that will be enough?"

Joanna was candid. "To be honest, it may not work. He may be very persistent, so I'll give you my phone number and if he rings again and you can't put him off give me a ring and I'll ring him."

"Oh, I couldn't involve you, could I? Would you mind? You know, I used to deal with problems every day when I was William's secretary; I don't know what has come over me. I'm getting old, I think."

"Nonsense! You just have a lot on your plate. And, to be honest, these people are intimidating. They con even the strongest men into parting with thousands. You're not alone – they're *con*men, Lily. But please, whatever you do, put him off. Don't let him bully you into giving him any money. Promise me."

"No, you're right," Lily agreed. "I'll just say Simon is going to deal with it as soon as he comes home and he has told me not to do anything until then."

"Right, good for you. Remember, you ate people like him for breakfast when you were a secretary. Now I'm going to give you my home phone number and if you need me for any reason, and I mean *any* reason, call or leave a message. We all check our messages so I will get it."

Holly had been showing William pictures from a book of country villages on the coffee table and he was more animated than Joanna had seen him before. Holly had such patience with him and he had really taken to her. His face had lit up when he saw her again.

They reluctantly said their goodbyes and left. Joanna would have to work a little faster if she intended to get the deliveries done on time.

The remainder of the day passed relatively without incident, but as Joanna pulled the little red van into the drive at the end of the day, nagging at the back of her mind were Lily and William, and their rogue roofers.

Tonight was Joanna's turn to cook, so, as she had had very little time to prepare anything in the morning, it was going to have to be something quick. Spag bol, she thought, that's fast. Then, as they always had loads of fruit in the house, what with Caribbean cuisine tending to use fruit in most recipes, she would throw together a fresh fruit salad for dessert. Joanna knew that she was cheating a bit as Alisha always made the most delicious desserts. However, she excused her tardiness with concern over William and Lily. Joanna hunted in the freezer for garlic bread and set the table. As if by magic, just as she had completed everything the phone rang.

"Don't worry, Lily. No, you haven't disturbed me, honestly. No, you haven't interrupted anything. Now tell me what's happened." Joanna kept her voice very calm so as to relax Lily, who was obviously upset but also sounded scared.

"Joanna, he threatened me," Lily wailed. "Oh, not in a violent way, but by what he was saying. He was warning me."

Joanna told Lily to stay calm and relay the story just as it had happened.

"Well, I had just given William his tray so that he could have his supper while he watched the news. I know he probably doesn't understand but I'm sure he likes it, and… Oh, sorry, I'm rambling, aren't I? Well, the telephone rang and I answered it, and it was the man about the roof, you know, the boss one. He asked if I had been to the bank for the money for the materials. He'd found he could fit me in tomorrow but he would need to buy the materials early in the morning so he was going to come round and collect the money this evening."

Lily's voice became more and more frantic as she relayed the conversation.

"I told him that I hadn't gone to the bank but that I had spoken to Simon, my son, and that he had told me not to bother because he would see to it when he came home. He wasn't very happy, I could tell by his voice. In fact, he became quite angry, in a cold voice sort of way, you know what I mean? He said he had put a good customer off for me so that as a special favour to me he could do my job first, as it was so urgent. Well, then I said again I was terribly sorry but my son Simon had said not to bother. I told him we would, of course, pay for the labour cost of the work yesterday.

"Oh, he really began to scare me. There was a long pause and then he said: 'Now, wait until I get this right… Well, I just hope your chimney stack doesn't come through your roof tonight as the weather is going to be worse again.' He said he would come round in the morning and we could have another little chat about the work he's done. 'Not forgetting that your husband signed the contract of work, agreeing to all the jobs…'"

Stunned, Lily told Joanna she'd had no idea that anyone had ever even been in the house and seen William. When she had spoken to the boss man they had stood in the passage. Then she said, "Oh wait, Joanna, I did go out with a tray of tea and biscuits for them, but that's beside the point. William hasn't written anything in years, it's almost impossible.

"Joanna, I'm afraid. There was something about his voice that made me think he was going to do something tonight so that I would be forced to have the work done by him. You were right – I may be retired but I'm not stupid, and I could sense the menace in his tone. Oh, Joanna, I'm sorry to bring this on you, a total stranger, but I don't know what to do. I couldn't tell the police, what would I say? A builder has offered to mend my roof and I have changed my mind and now I'm afraid."

"Actually, Lily," counselled Joanna, "you would probably find they would be more sympathetic than you think, but we won't take the chance. I know what you mean about your story sounding a bit 'out there', especially if you tell them Holly's role in all this. But I know Holly is never wrong and I am more convinced than ever now, so listen: this is what I am going to do. I am going to come over now and I have a plan. Do you have a sleeping bag?"

"Erm, yes! What on earth for?"

"I'll tell you when I get there. Don't worry, we will sort this out. Try not to get stressed. You are not alone, okay?"

"Oh, thank you, Joanna. I don't know where I would have been without your kindness."

Joanna assured Lily that it was rubbish and she was glad she could help. Then she explained to Alisha and the girls where she was going, telling them not to worry, that she wouldn't be doing anything strong arm or tackling any burglars. She just wanted to reassure Lily that she wasn't alone.

"I know what you are like, Joanna. If only Joel were here."

The girls looked at one another after seeing what Alisha had said. They laughed a little uncertainly, though, understanding the gravity of the situation. Although it was funny to think that Joel could help in any way, it was worrying that Joanna was going to tackle this man alone.

"Oh for goodness sake, I'm not tackling anyone, and I'm not alone. Lily and William are there. I just can't leave Lily alone to worry all night on her own. It's probably just a threat so that in the morning when he calls she will give in and go to the bank for the money. I promise all concerned that if anything, *anything* at all happens I will ring the police. I have my mobile and it's charged so that even if I'm tied up and can't get to the house phone… I'm kidding, I'm kidding!" Joanna said quickly as they all started to get very worried expressions on their faces. Holly said it was all her fault because if she hadn't seen the horrible men this wouldn't have happened and her mum wouldn't be taking burglars on single-handed.

"Oh for goodness sake, no one is taking burglars on single-handed and, Holly, you did the right thing and I'm proud of you. Imagine what would have happened if you hadn't overheard their conversation. Poor William and Lily would be facing this on their own, or paying out lots of money for work that doesn't need doing. Goodness knows where it would have stopped.

"Now, I've got to go, and please don't worry. I'll ring you when I know anything, but you'd better not ring me or I'll probably have a heart attack, okay?"

Chapter 4

When Joanna arrived at the station she decided
to park the van round the back, out of sight of
the old station house and ticket office, where
there was a large U-shaped parking area from
times past. She had brought with her the lamp
she wore on her head in the dark mornings, so
that she could see the addresses on the mail,
and also a large torch. She wasn't entirely sure
of her plan yet, other than that she intended to
hide somewhere and lie in wait in case anyone
tried to climb the ladder and do something
dodgy to the chimney, just to give Lily enough
of a scare to pay the money. Part of Joanna
thought how ridiculous this all was, but the
other half could not deny what Holly had seen
the rogues discussing.

She knocked at the front door, and it was
evident that poor Lily must have been sat on
the chair in the hall waiting for her coming.
This must have been a bit of a nightmare for
the couple: they already had William's
condition to cope with, and now Lily had this
and a whopping great plaster on her foot.
Joanna felt sure, if it was her, she would have
been scared out of her wits.

Once Joanna was inside, Lily again apologised for 'being a bother', and Joanna had to assure her that she was nothing of the sort and that it was her social duty. She hated people who did this type of thing to elderly people, stopping herself just in time from saying 'old', as she didn't think Lily would've appreciated that at all. She still appeared very sprightly, well, as much as she could with a plaster pot on her foot and a stick to help support her.

As they went into the living room, William automatically looked behind Joanna, to see if Holly was coming. Joanna went over to William and looked directly at his upturned face, saying clearly but gently that she hadn't brought Holly tonight as it was rather late but that he would see her tomorrow. She reached down and brushed the back of his hand. He seemed to understand and went back to staring into the flames of the open fire.

"Okay, Lily, do you have that sleeping bag?"

Lily bustled to get it and held it out as though it was going to perform a magic trick.

Joanna explained her quickly formed plan. "Is there an outside coal house or something where I can see anyone arriving and with a view with access to the roof where the tiles have been ripped off?"

"Oh yes, there is the woodshed just opposite."

"Great. I suppose I could pile some wood up and sit on it." Joanna spoke to herself, thinking out loud.

Lily offered, "There's the wooden settle that Simon uses to chop the logs on. That's in there. It's hard, but it's better than stacking wood. What are you going to do, Joanna?"

Again Lily remonstrated with herself for getting Joanna involved in anything dangerous. After all, Joanna had a daughter to look out for and she shouldn't be worrying about silly old people with broken ankles and dementia.

"Now listen here, Lily," Joanna said firmly, "you are not silly old people. You are people who need someone to help you at this time, that's all. You are not stupid, or incapable, but at the moment you are slightly incapacitated with your ankle and William, bless him, can't help, but I can. I won't do anything dangerous if anyone comes and attempts to climb on the roof. I will simply call the police, but I must see their faces to know it's definitely the men who claim to be mending your roof, et cetera. Now, will you stop worrying?

"As for the plan, there is no point in rushing out yet because I don't think they will come before bedtime. Is the ladder still outside?"

"Yes. They didn't take it because they were coming back to do more work. Why?"

"Just an idea. Now, shall we all have a nice cup of coffee and just stay calm and relax for a little while?"

The time seemed to drag by and, even though Joanna would never usually be in bed before eleven, by ten o'clock she was really flagging and so was William. He had no idea that anything was wrong. Joanna suggested that Lily got William into bed, put the lights out that she would normally put out at this time of night, then relaxed for a while on the sofa.

"What are you going to do?" Lily asked.

Joanna thought it a bit early but she was sure that if she didn't leave Lily to rest she would be a physical wreck in the morning and she had William to take care of. "Do you have a flask, Lily?"

Giving Lily something to do helped take her mind off the situation. She filled a flask with black coffee and gave it to Joanna.

"Are you sure about this, Joanna? I wouldn't think any the less of you if you 'chickened out', don't they say?"

"Ha ha, yes, that's what they say, but don't worry: I have no intentions of chickening out. Right, I'm off outside. All I want you to do is pretend you don't hear a thing. Honestly, there is no reason why you should have to be bothered. If anything happens I am simply going to shine the light in his face and tell him I have taken a photo. I'm sure that will scare him off. I'll shout if I need your help. Other than that, do not come outside, okay?"

"I promise," said Lily.

After Lily had pointed out the woodshed and given Joanna the sleeping bag and flask,

Joanna used her torch to find her way into her hiding place. She was a little excited, yet could not help also being a tad nervous. She hadn't even thought about taking a photo until just then, when it had popped into her mind as a way of reassuring Lily.

Joanna had found the wooden bench to sit on. She climbed inside the sleeping bag to keep warm, but didn't zip it up. She had visions of falling out of the woodshed door, tripping up inside the sleeping bag like in the sack race at school. She had her elasticated lamp around her head and her phone in her hand. Now all she had to do was wait, without falling asleep. Isn't it amazing, she thought: you would never have believed that anyone could fall asleep in a woodshed while waiting for a baddie to arrive! You would think your heart would be racing and your head thumping, but, apart from her rear end being rather numb from sitting on the hard wooden settle, she could have dozed off nicely. After all, she had been up since five thirty that morning.

She had instructed Lily to turn off all the usual lights, so it would appear that they had gone to bed, which she had. So, apart from the odd hoot of an owl, everything was dark and quiet. She settled down for a long wait. The wind had started to get a little gusty – not as bad as the night before but it was still a night when you wanted to be snuggled up under the duvet, not sitting in a woodshed with goodness knows what crawling about.

She didn't have to wait long before she heard a door slam. A car or a van? thought Joanna. Then her heart really did start thumping in her chest when she heard footsteps, coming closer and closer, crunching on the gravel.

She gently parted the door of the woodshed just a crack, so she could see if the person was going towards the house. Sure enough, he was walking straight towards it. He stopped at the ladder and dropped something that looked like a tool bag. Joanna wriggled free of the sleeping bag, holding her breath and concentrating on ways of opening the shed door without any noise, so she could shine her torch and try to take a photo all at the same time. Damn, she thought, I need another hand.

How am I going to do this? She decided to put the torch down on the ground and just use the one on her head, so that she would have her hands free to take the photo.

She managed to creep gently out of the shed without the door making a sound. She had one hand over the lamp on her head so it wouldn't shine until she was close enough to take the snap. The figure had put one hand on either side of the ladder, probably just about to climb up on to the roof, when Joanna took her hand off her head lamp with a flourish and attempted to press her camera on her phone while at the same time grabbing his legs so that he would be shocked enough to turn around and be full face to the camera.

Well, that was the theory anyway. The next thing Joanna knew she was being pinned down by what felt like The Hulk. She wriggled incessantly, but couldn't get either one of her arms free to help herself. She felt as though her head had been hit with a hammer as it had whacked against the ground from the sheer force of the man's weight.

Her voice eventually came to her and, realising now was not the time to be quiet any more, she shouted at the great brute of a man who had the whole of his what felt like twenty stone forcing her to the ground and into submission.

"What the hell? What the bloody hell is going on? Put that bloody light out of my eyes."

All Joanna could see was his screwed-up eyes, but she had the strange feeling that anyone who spoke as he did, even if it was to curse, couldn't be the kind of person she was lying in wait for.

Also there was something about the smell of him that made her have her doubts. This man smelt very nice. Fleetingly, she thought she even recognised his cologne as something Joel used.

"Get off me. You're hurting me, you great oaf, let me up!" Joanna began to get frantic; the feeling of helplessness was not something she cared for. "Let me up and I'll turn the light off, but only if you tell me who you are and what you're doing here at this time of night attempting to climb on to the roof of this house?"

"This is my house and, never mind that, what were you doing jumping out of the dark with a flashlight on your head and a ladder against the roof of my house?"

Just then the front door opened and light flooded out from the hall. There stood Lily with what looked like a rolling pin in one hand and her stick in the other. She hobbled over to the couple lying on the ground.

"You better leave her alone. I have called the police and they are on their way so you better skedaddle, I mean it," said good old Lily in her most ferocious voice, a credit to any am dram performance of a Miss Marple thriller.

"Mother, what the hell?"

"Simon? Simon? Is that you? What are you doing?"

"Never mind that! What are you doing? Do you know this woman?"

"Erm, do you think you could get up now?" gasped Joanna. "You are suffocating me; I can't breathe with your weight on my chest."

"Oh, I'm sorry. Now, what the hell is going on?"

But just then the noise of a truck could be heard and Joanna said, "Shh, listen." Then, "Shush," she said again as the famous Simon was going to open his mouth. "I'll explain in a minute," she whispered.

The flat-bed truck belonging to the roofing company, or rogues, as they were known to Lily and Joanna, swung into the yard. They were just about to stop when they obviously caught sight of the small group, which stood out, with the light from the passage illuminating the scene perfectly. The driver of the truck could not do a three-point turn quickly enough and sped off into the distance.

"Damn!" said Joanna.

"Blast!" said Lily.

"Mother!" said Simon, shocked at his mother's language and apparent involvement in some sort of skulduggery, at her age and with a pot on her ankle. "Will someone please tell me what the hell is going on?"

"Oh, Simon, it is lovely to see you, but I wish you hadn't arrived at this particular time. We might have caught them if you had only arrived half an hour later."

"Oh, I give up. I came because you seemed to be having a rotten time at the moment, what with your foot, and some ridiculous problem with the roof, which I very much doubt, Mother, because I had it all done recently, as you well know. And now it would appear I have come at the wrong time."

"Please let poor Joanna get to her feet and we will go inside and explain it all to you, over a stiff drink."

Simon more or less hoisted Joanna up from her prone position. She rubbed the back of her head where she had whacked it on the gravelled drive and he dusted gravel from his clothes. By the time they were sat down in the warmth, Simon and Lily had a reviving glass in their hands and Joanna had a black coffee, as she still had to drive home after all the excitement.

Lily explained what had happened, how Holly had read the lips of the 'villains', as Lily put it. Although Simon was sceptical about the lip reading, Lily assured him, saying, "You have to meet her, Simon, she is amazing, and your father has really taken to her. He almost comes to life when he sees her." There was real warmth in her voice.

Simon's face showed even more signs of scepticism. He carried on in his irritated yet controlled voice, saying that the roof was perfect, and that the chimney stack had been done the last time he was home. "You must remember that, Mum?"

"Simon, I don't know what on earth you do when you are home. I never really take much notice and I'm so busy looking after your father it goes in one ear and out of the other. If you told me I just didn't listen. I'm sorry. If I'd listened this wouldn't have happened and Joanna wouldn't have put herself at risk." Lily's voice cracked as though any minute she would burst into tears with the shear strain of it all.

Joanna took over the explanation, telling Lily to have a swig of her drink while she described what the supposed roofing company had done initially and then how they were trying to get Lily to go to the bank and withdraw two thousand pounds for materials and labour.

"What?" Simon said, getting angry and feeling totally helpless at having been absent when his mother needed him.

Joanna continued, saying, "Well, we were up to their scam—"

Lily cut in, "Joanna told me to tell them I had been in touch with you and that you had said just to leave it until you got home and you would tend to it. I said we would pay them for the work they had carried out. But they didn't like that and they said the chimney stack might fall through the roof tonight as the weather was going to be bad and I didn't know what to do so Joanna was trying to help me and it's all my fault." Lily's voice began to crack again, so Joanna took over the story once more. She could see Simon clearly now under the living room lights. And her abiding thought was that she had been lying underneath him in the station yard and hadn't realised how…very male he was, although she recalled he did smell very masculine.

Concentrate, she chided herself, although it was hard to simply ignore the fact that her stomach was doing some sort of summersault. Even though the danger had passed now, she was sure it wasn't that. Trying again to marshal her thoughts, she acknowledged the fact that he was very, very attractive. The uniform completely did it for her. Concentrate she said again to herself, you see men every day in uniform. That was only loosely true, though, as they were postmen's uniforms and not exactly in the same league. Joanna dragged her scrambled mind back to the business in hand.

"I thought if I could catch them in the act of tampering with the chimney stack by maybe taking a photograph of them I could… Well… Confront them with it and threaten to take them to the police if they didn't leave your mother and father alone." Joanna tapered off under the sceptical stare from the darkest eyes she had ever seen. Her face instantly flushed as she realised that she was practically gawping like a teenager with her tongue hanging out.

As Joanna composed herself, and pulled her thoughts back to the events of the evening, she said, "When you arrived and I saw you with your hands on the ladder, I thought you were him, coming back to tamper with the chimney. So I sneaked up on you and, well, you know the rest. How was I to know you would be coming home?"

"Yes, Simon, if I had known you were coming home, I could have told the men the truth. I thought you couldn't get away? When I phoned you, you said how busy you were."

"I am. I was," Simon answered. "I managed to swap with another pilot. You were trying to sound so brave, what with your ankle and Dad, so I knew you must be struggling to cope, but would never admit it. What on earth were you doing on the bloody roof in the first place anyway?"

Lily told him, "It all started with one tile that was sticking out and I thought all I had to do was push it back in and I did. But I slipped and the rest is history. The roofing people must have seen the ladder against the roof and taken the opportunity to offer their services to some silly old biddy with a broken ankle."

"God, I'll have the law on them," Simon fumed. "Just wait until they try it again, I'll kill them. God, it's getting so that decent people can't just get on with their lives. Isn't it bad enough you have to cope with Dad, but to have to cope with despicable crooks? Have you got their address? I'll have the police involved first thing in the morning. I'll see them in court for this."

"Well, the problem is, Simon," said Lily, "I didn't know this, but while I was taking a tray with tea for the workers outside, one of them, the boss, I think, got your father to sign a contract of some sort. I think they will still demand money for the work they said we needed doing."

"A contract? Dad signed a piece of paper? Dad hasn't signed anything in years. It's impossible; they must have forged it. Oh my God, this is ridiculous. I don't believe this is happening. Well, that makes my mind up: once I sort this out we are moving."

"Moving? What do you mean moving? Where to?"

"I'm going to do what I have talked about for years, set up my own freight service. I should have done it years ago. I've been toying with it a lot lately, and I'm fed up with commercial flights. That's what I came home to tell you: I've taken a month's leave in order to find the right type of airfield and hangars that I'll need to run the business from. This just makes it clearer. We can't stay here and you can't manage Dad on your own. I don't mean that in a disdainful way, Mum. I know you have done it ever since Dad had his stroke, or his illness, whatever they call it, and you have done a great job. But look what happens when something happens to you." Simon indicated Lily's plaster cast. "You need someone to help you. I can do that much better if I am working from home."

Joanna stood up to go, as this was none of her business, and it would appear they didn't need her now. She wondered how on earth she was going to get up for work in the morning or even if it was worth going to bed at all.

"Oh, Joanna, I'm terribly sorry. We are talking away, forgetting you've got to go to work in the morning. I can never thank you – *we* can never thank you enough, can we, Simon?"

"No, Mum's right, we are very grateful to you, Joanna, is it?"

"No, it's nothing, really, but I have a feeling this isn't over yet. I hope it is but if anything comes of the so-called contract will you let me see it? Maybe I can do something about it."

"Well, that's very kind of you, but unless you are a solicitor I can't imagine you being able to do anything I won't be able to. And, to be honest, I'm in favour of taking them to court or breaking bones, one or the other."

Joanna was in no doubt that he was more than capable, but whether that was the solution or not, she didn't think so.

"But I am very grateful for your help," Simon continued. "I'll see you to your car. I would drive you home but I haven't had time to hire a car yet. I arrived by taxi."

"Ah, taxi, that's what the thud was, the taxi door. I thought it was the truck."

Lily put her hand on Joanna's arm, thanking her profusely, again and again, telling her to have a good night's sleep ready for work and that she would see her tomorrow, reminding her to drive carefully, that things always seem worse late at night. As Simon and Joanna went into the chilled night air, Joanna remembered her torch in the woodshed and they almost tripped over Simon's holdall. Oh, thought Joanna, his bag... She'd thought it had been the burglar's toolkit.

"Where is your car?" Simon looked around curiously.

"Round the back. I hid it; we didn't want anyone to know that I was here. We thought we had covered everything. Actually we had."

"You are both absolutely mad. What would have happened if I really had been one of the men? You could have been seriously hurt, you know that, don't you?" Simon's voice was angry. He didn't exactly know whom to be angry with, but one thing he was grateful for was that he had decided to come home tonight and not wait until tomorrow as planned.

As they turned the corner, Simon was looking for a car, not really comprehending that the little red van was it! He looked puzzled as Joanna walked towards it with her key in her hand.

"What the…? Is this yours? Is this your car? Is it for real? I mean, a real post van, is that your job?"

"Yes," said Joanna defensively, sticking her chin up and giving it her whole five feet seven inches, proudly saying yes, she was a postwoman.

"Well, excuse me for stating the obvious, but how on earth do you expect to be able to help my mother with a contract, always supposing there is one, which I doubt?"

"Well, I only offered my services to help your parents, and I know a little about the law, as I have recently qualified in social care and law. But if you don't want my help then I recommend you get in touch with a solicitor, that's always supposing they get in touch, which they may not."

With that Joanna climbed into her van and drove off, leaving him standing in the dark. She could see in her reversing mirror that he stood until she had actually left the station yard and was on the road.

Chapter 5

As Joanna drove through the darkness and the empty streets she knew so well, she had time to recap on the night's fiasco, mentally recalling the events in order to decide if her and Lily's actions had been purely foolhardy, as Simon quite clearly thought, or if indeed they were justified. If so, would she do it again? The answer was a resounding yes, she would do it again. However, she was rather glad that she hadn't been grappling with a real burglar on the hard, gravelled drive.

To be honest, she reasoned, what else could she have done differently? True, waiting in the woodshed was a bit 'Famous Five-ish'. Maybe she should have gone to the police with her suspicions. Despite what she had told Lily about them being more sympathetic than she imagined, though, she didn't think that they would have done anything until money had changed hands, and possible menaces had been inferred. By that time it would have been too late: Lily and William would have been sucked in and left feeling silly. Knowing them now, Joanna was aware they would have been unwilling to seek any kind of help.

Joanna often read in the papers that elderly people who had been in the same position as Lily and William and who had lost most of their life savings were usually too embarrassed to tell anyone. God knew why, it certainly wasn't anything they had done wrong; it was probably the feeling that they had been taken in, something they link with 'geriatric behaviour'. Which is ridiculous, thought Joanna, we've all bought something similar – a dress, a carpet, a car – where we've been taken in and the goods haven't been what we thought, but we accept it as a learning experience. Unfortunately as soon as it involves older people there is the stigma of 'geriatric incompetence'.

Pulling into the drive in the dark and quietly closing the van door, Joanna thought she would sneak into the house and upstairs to bed without waking any of the household.

However, that was never going to happen. As she put her key in the door and crept into the passage, stealthily walking towards the stairs, a sudden burst of light and voices broke the silence of the night.

"What happened?"

"Why are you so late?"

"Did you grapple with any burglars?" This last was said by Holly and Precious in unison with an air of expectancy and trepidation.

Joanna held up both hands, attempting to put this off until the next morning as she was so tired. She explained that she had to be up early in order to collect her deliveries. However, that was also a no-no; she was going to tell the whole tale or she would never get to bed.

Joanna relayed it just as it happened, but also had to contend with and fend off constant questions about her 'grappling' with what she thought was a burglar. Was she scared? Would she have got the better of him? Both these questions were put by Holly and Precious, of course. Joel was simply glad that nothing serious had happened and Alisha wanted to know what 'this Simon' looked like.

"I must go to bed now," Joanna said in an effort to avoid any questions about Simon. She wasn't able to form any thoughts about him herself, yet. "I'm shattered. Holly, are you coming with me in the morning as it's the last day of your holidays?"

"Yes. I want to see if William is all right, and see Lily, of course."

"Okay, well, we better all get to sleep."

Everyone reluctantly made their way back up to bed. The girls were signing at great speed, the excitement etched on their faces. Alisha was giving Joel knowing looks and smiles.

Lying in her lovely warm bed Joanna should have fallen off to sleep like a log. She had even felt like sleeping when she had been sat on the hard bench in the woodshed. So surely it couldn't just be the excitement of the night, although few normal people could simply come home and go to sleep after an event like tonight. She wondered how policemen were when they got home. Much the same, she thought. But Joanna was reluctant to admit that the reason she was still feeling this buzz of adrenalin was that it wasn't often you found yourself lying underneath a very large chunk of man, trying not to think about how handsome he was. She may as well simply get up and go to work in the middle of the night as she would never sleep at all.

Eventually she dropped off, but when her alarm clock went off at her usual time, for the first time since the deep dark days of February she felt like switching it off and turning over. However, she dragged herself up, having a very quick shower and dressing in her usual uniform. She went in to give Holly a shove. Holly was wonderful at getting up – no matter what time it was, she woke up as bright as a button and just as happy. In fact, she was a morning tonic.

After collecting the mail and starting her deliveries Joanna had recovered her usual cheerful manner, with all the early risers who liked to greet her at the door waving to Holly in the van. By the time they reached Lily and William's, the sun was shining and it was going to be a lovely autumn day.

Holly could hardly contain her excitement; her usual reserve had most definitely been overcome by her sudden affection for Lily and William. As Holly hurried up the long drive the front door opened and Lily was smiling at them both saying, "Come in, come in. You must have time for a coffee, please."

Actually, Joanna had her favourites where she usually did stop for a coffee, and places where she simply sat to enjoy the beauty of the scenery, so she did have time. As they got into the lounge, William looked towards the door and Holly went over to greet him with her usual radiant smile, holding out her hand towards him. It was truly amazing to anyone that knew William and knew there had been none or very little expression on his pale face since his stroke, and yet there was definitely a hint of a smile and there was no mistaking the fact that he lifted his hand in an effort to take Holly's in his.

As Holly sat on the floor beside William she signed and spoke to Lily, asking about the excitement of the night.

"Were you scared? How did Mum tackle the man? Oh, I wish I had been here to see it. Did William see it?"

"Ha, ha, no, dear, William was safely tucked up in bed as it was rather late when it all happened. And yes, I was scared. I got my rolling pin from the kitchen and I would have hit the man on the head if he had hurt your mother."

"It's a good job you didn't; you would have brained me," said a voice from the doorway. As they turned towards the door, Holly followed them with her gaze.

Lily said, "Oh, Simon, did we wake you? Sorry, we were just telling Holly all about our adventure last night."

Simon remained standing in the doorway, dressed in what looked like a navy blue towelling robe and very little else underneath, Joanna guessed. His dark hair was dishevelled and he had a slight dark growth of beard. He seemed to have no idea how heart-wrenchingly gorgeous he looked to a woman who had been totally, absolutely and, almost, happily celibate for years.

"Holly, this is Simon. Simon is my son."

Bless her, Lily rounded each syllable so that Holly would understand every word. Holly gave one of her most radiant smiles – you could almost hear a sigh from most of the people she met. Simon was no different. Being a man, he didn't make a big thing about it, but Joanna could see that his total body language was that of someone who was genuinely happy to meet such a pleasant and pretty child.

"Hello, my name is Holly. Mum said she 'grappled on the ground with you, thinking you were the villain'," said Holly, signing and speaking with great excitement in her slightly monotone voice, the only outward sign she was deaf.

Simon was definitely enchanted by this little girl, and her smile, which was contagious, had its usual effect, reducing the recipient to mush. "Well, hello. I can assure you, young lady, I am not a villain, although I know I look a bit like a pirate this morning."

Referring to his beard and dishevelled look, making Holly laugh, he continued, "It's not my fault. Blame that on your mother and mine for their madcap scheme, and attacking me when I arrived home in all innocence in the dark. Then a mad woman launched herself at me with a torch shining in my eyes. It could have been an alien for all I knew. Now what would you think?"

Simon was outrageously encouraging Holly to join in the blame game against both their parents. However, he was flogging a dead horse there, as Holly thought her mother so courageous and cool for not being like a stodgy parent. Usually people said things should be left to the authorities. Instead Joanna jumped in with both feet, which to an eight-year-old was definitely cool.

"Oh, Mum's not scared; she would tackle anything. She is going to fight in the courts now she has her degree, and she is going to stand up for all the little people who can't speak for themselves. Aren't you, Mum?" Holly signed and spoke with the fierce determination and innocence of a child.

William watched Holly speaking and signing with a look that could only be described as wonder, as though he had heard some of what she had said and even registered it. That was pure fancy, of course; how could he? He hadn't been in contact with the outside world for three years, since the day of his stroke.

Holly went over and held William's hand and smiled at him. There was no doubt that his mouth changed shape and it was as though he would break into a smile at any minute. He didn't, but Holly was not put off. She would continue as though coaching a shy person to smile.

Simon watched in utter amazement. He turned to his mother and Joanna, saying, "You know last night when you told me why you set about your madcap scheme, and based on whose evidence? I must admit I was sceptical but... She is a remarkable child."

Then he seemed to recover his sterner attitude to the situation, telling them again that they were absolutely foolish and irresponsible to attempt to sort the situation out themselves.

"Irresponsible? I beg your pardon, I don't agree. How do you make that out?" Lily demanded.

"Well, Mother, for a start you have Dad to think about. And you…err, Joanna," Simon was not sure about using her Christian name as he didn't even know the woman. "What would have happened if anything had happened to you? You have your daughter to think about. She is your first priority, not roofs and villains."

"So you think I should just have let them take advantage of your parents? Take their money and not help? Not tell what Holly had seen? Is that what you think?" Joanna's voice became heated and higher than normal.

Holly was not aware at first, as she had her back to her, but she turned around and could sense by the grown-ups' faces that things were not right.

"Mum, what is it?"

"Simon thinks we shouldn't have told Lily and William about the bad men, Holly. What do you think?"

"I'm sorry; it's my fault for telling Mum what they said, but I couldn't let William and Lily sit in the house with the water coming in the roof. The men did it on purpose; I saw them, honestly I did."

Simon immediately felt contrite at being caught out losing his temper because he was worried, because he felt impotent at not being in two places at once.

Simon knelt down to Holly's level. As much as Joanna tried not to look, her eyes were drawn to the gap where his dressing gown precariously covered his essentials. She had to concentrate on what he was saying to Holly, which was that she had been right in what she had told her mum and that he was very grateful that the villains had not got away with their scam because of her quick thinking. He was simply feeling very guilty for not being here to protect his parents. Holly accepted this and, turning to William, told him he would be fine because she would look after him, although she wouldn't see him for a while because she was back at school on Monday.

Simon touched Holly's shoulder so that she knew he was talking to her, as though he spoke to the deaf on a regular basis. He asked her which school she went to and Holly replied, "I go to the Royal School for the Deaf, but I would like to go to a normal school next year when I am nine."

Holly looked hopefully at her mum, who said she and Holly were currently in discussion about that. This was said with a finality that warned Holly not to pursue it in company and at this time.

A quick look at her watch made Joanna realise that they should be pushing on soon. She repeated that, if they got a letter or any contact from the roofing people, her offer of help was still open, acknowledging that now Simon was home they probably wouldn't need her.

Lily thanked Joanna again and said that now they were friends she would be really grateful if they would call in and have coffee with her any time they were passing. And she hoped Holly could come, as she was such a comfort to William. She had definitely noticed a change in William's behaviour.

Simon and Lily saw Joanna and Holly to the door and Holly waved goodbye to William.

Again his thin smile was evident to those who knew him.

Joanna, waving, said she would see them tomorrow, Saturday, and then was having a few days' holiday. As they drove off she could see Simon still standing on the doorstep, looking sexy in his towelling robe. It seemed she was destined to read his expressions through her rear-view mirror. Whatever was she thinking, becoming interested in someone she didn't even know simply because he set her hormones in a tizzy?

Holly was saying what a nice man Simon was and Joanna said, in an absent sort of distracted tone, "Erm, yesss, I suppose he is." Holly didn't actually have to hear that to know there was something strange about what her mum had said and the expression on her face as she said it. She rolled her eyes in a way that meant she couldn't wait to get home and tell Precious.

Chapter 6

Joanna was home in good time to have a quick coffee with Alisha before she went off to work at the hospital on the late shift. This meant that Joanna would give the girls tea as the grown-ups usually had a very late evening meal together when both Joel and Alisha were working late.

Joanna, feeling less tired, decided to catch up on some housework. As Alisha had finished all the washing and ironing, Joanna would do the hoovering and polishing throughout. It was a fairly substantial house, but, considering they all had busy lives, everything ran pretty smoothly on the whole.

When Joanna put her head around Precious's bedroom door to warn the girls of the oncoming vacuum, she could tell by their coy expressions that they had been discussing something they didn't particularly want her to hear. However, their giggles could be heard in the street: there were lots of 'oohs' and ahs' followed by squeals of pure delight, and rolling around the bedroom floor in fits of laughter.

"Well, what on earth has set you two off? I can hear you all the way downstairs. Now it couldn't be that I was going to ask you to help me tidy up, because I'm sure that would send you into raptures."

Holly and Precious, with her huge round eyes and expressive face framed by jet black, tight curly hair meticulously plaited into strips and fastened to her head, looked as though their pure excitement was about to make them burst.

Then Holly said to her mum, "I was telling Precious about William's son Simon, how nice he was, and how he said he looked like a pirate. Did you think he looked like a pirate, Mummy?"

Joanna dragged the Hoover into the bedroom and started to pick things up off the floor, stopping in the midst of what she was doing with a distant expression on her face while she visualised Simon as a pirate.

This delighted the girls, who squealed, winked and pushed each other with a 'see, what did I tell you?' look.

"Well, yesss, I suppose he did, but he was probably just tired and in need of a shave."

Joanna came to her senses and saw what the girls were leading up to. The next question would have been how did she like Simon; and did she think he was good-looking? She quickly flipped the switch off the vacuum, telling them to jump up on the bed or they would be sucked up. Normally a vacuum cleaner noise would stop any conversation stone dead. However, it didn't matter in the slightest if you happened to be deaf, so Joanna deliberately averted her eyes, which soon stopped the questions.

She rattled away hoovering the floor, throwing soft toys on to their beds. She threw the duster towards them on the bed and lifted her head only long enough to say, "Thank you," meaning, 'Dust, please'.

The housework done, the girls' tea over and done with, and the evening meal ongoing, Joanna decided to have a long hot soak in the bath. It seemed as though she had just laid her head on the back of the bath when she saw the light flashing on the phone, meaning there was an incoming call. In a house where there were deaf occupants, little things such as getting the phone for someone while they were in the bath didn't happen. It was one of those unfortunate irritations that you were never off duty even in the bathroom, and there was a phone and a doorbell light in every room.

"Damn, you wouldn't credit it. You cannot even take a bloody bath at…," glancing at her watch on the side of the bath, "eight o'clock in the evening. If this is a call about double glazing I will blast *them* out of the water, instead of me."

Joanna leaned almost out of the bath to grab the phone off the wall and then sloshed back into the warm, bubble-filled bath.

"Hello, Joanna Berry."

There was a slight pause before a familiar voice said, "Joanna, it's Simon Winter."

Another pause, giving Joanna time to digest this unexpected information.

"Yes, Simon, how can I help you?"

"I hope I'm not disturbing you?"

"No, no, it's fine. I'm just, well, never mind, what can I do for you?" Joanna said, instinctively covering her chest with her free hand just in case he could see down the phone.

"Well, it's as you predicted. There was a letter hand-posted through the door today and it was from the roofing company saying they want to either continue with the work, or for work already carried out they want three thousand pounds plus VAT. *Plus* VAT, would you believe?

"Actually, I want to go to the address and punch their lights out. I fully intended to hire a car for a few weeks while I'm home, but I cannot find my driving licence and it would appear, no matter how many hire companies I ring, they will not entertain me without a current licence. So, to cut a long story short, and say no if you have plans, did you say you had a few days' holiday starting on Monday?"

"Erm, yes, yes I did, and no, I wasn't going away or anything. What do you need?"

"Well, firstly, I need to hire a car and I wondered if we could hire it in your name? I know this is a real imposition and you have done more than enough for my parents, but I cannot get a replacement licence in time. You see, I have some addresses of properties I would like to look at with the intention of starting up on my own. I know this sounds like a great way to start, losing my driving licence, but I can only tell you I am a better pilot than the impression you have of me at present."

"Erm, you have caught me on the hop, so to speak, but yes, erm, that shouldn't be a problem. I will need to check with my friends, Alisha and Joel, but I will let you know for definite in the morning."

"Oh, you were going out with your friends? I'm sorry."

"No, no, not going out. Joel and Alisha are the family we house share with, Holly and I. Joel is a doctor and Alisha is a nurse so they work shifts but I will double-check and I'll see you in the morning at the usual time when I come to your parents'. I don't think there will be a problem."

"Thank you, Joanna, I am very grateful."

The phone went click and that was it. Joanna lay back in the speedily cooling bath water, knowing there would be no way she would relax now so she may as well get out. She quickly dressed in her cosy dressing gown on hearing the front door bang, which heralded Joel. She could hear his conversation start and wondered if Alisha was with him or if he was talking to himself, as he often did.

She shouted that she would be down in a minute, then Alisha called up, "No hurry, we are having a glass of wine. Would you like one?"

Joanna shouted yes and ran a comb quickly through her thick, wavy hair, which didn't seem to need much attention and luckily always looked well groomed.

"Hi, dinners ready, just needs putting on the table. How's things with you both? The girls are in bed, although they may not be asleep yet."

"I'm fine and dandy," said Joel, looking very tired and thanking his lucky stars he had five days off.

Alisha joked, "Why can we never arrange our days off so that we are all off together? I don't believe it. I'm off on Wednesday and Thursday."

"Well," Joel said, "we will have Wednesday, my darling. What shall we do with the whole day together?" He rolled his eyes suggestively and wiggled his fingers in her direction, "And the girls are back at school…"

Alisha slipped out of his grasping fingers, laughing. "Down boy, dinner is ready."

"I would rather eat you, my sexy wife," he said in another attempt to catch her.

"Look," Alisha joked, "he is so tired he can't even catch me, so what on earth does he think he is going to do with me when he does?"

The general laughter ensued as they enjoyed the supper and the wine.

"Oh, I'm not sure," Joanna began, "but I may have to prevail upon your days off yet. I'm not sure but Simon called tonight…"

"Simon called? *The* Simon? The 'yum, yum Simon', as the girls are calling him, called here tonight?"

"He phoned, he did not call. That is his problem: he cannot go anywhere because he has lost his driving licence somewhere and he needs to hire a car and they will not let him without a valid licence. To top the lot, they have had a hand-delivered letter from the roofing company. Do you know they have asked for three thousand pounds on top of the work they've signed a contract for? Simon would like to go round and punch them on the nose, but he can't very well arrive in a taxi then stand and wait while his return taxi collects him in order to make his fast getaway, now, can he? So he has asked me if we can hire a car in my name… And he wants to look at some property while he is here but I'm not sure what that's all about. I said I would let him know in the morning. So," said Joanna with a pleading look, "is there any chance that I can prevail upon my favourite housemates in case I am needed elsewhere? I will even take the girls shopping at the mall tomorrow afternoon when I finish work for their new school shoes. How's that?"

"Shall we?" Joel looked to his wife. "What else could we get out of this bargain, Alisha? Should we make her Hoover right through the house?"

"It's done."

"Erm, should we make you empty the bin bags?"

"Done."

"Damn, it looks like she's got us, Lish. Oh, all right then, you can have your favour. What was it again?" said Joel in his good-natured way. Joanna said she wasn't sure yet but she thought she may end up taxiing Simon around until they could sort out the roofing company and the hire car.

"Not a problem," Joel said in his wonderful Caribbean accent.

Joanna said her goodnights and took her glass of wine up to bed. She had had a thought over dinner that there must be a loophole in this contract that William had supposedly signed, which would stop this ridiculous situation in its tracks. She really didn't want Lily and Simon to have to have this hanging over them for the short time he was home. Lily quite obviously needed to enjoy Simon being home and this wasn't helping anyone. Joanna sorted through a pile of her law books and found the ones she thought might help, then propped herself up in bed and began to wade through them. She would find the answer if it killed her. However, it would probably be the lack of sleep that finished her off as she set her clock for work in the morning with the distinct pleasure of knowing she was on holiday from Sunday, and tomorrow was her last day.

Chapter 7

Joanna was feeling very pleased with herself and had no trouble getting up for work that morning, even though she had managed very little sleep. In fact, she could hardly sleep after she got that Eureka moment. Lying in bed, swamped in books, in this case it had involved nothing more than a 'point of law' to give her the best feeling she had had in bed for a very long time.

Hurrying through her round this morning with a feeling of real excitement, she didn't examine the feeling too closely, or she may have had to question her motive for the turbulent feeling she could barely contain. Was it simply that she thought she had the answer to Lily and William's problem? Or could it be anything to do with the fact that Simon needed her, and, for whatever reason, she would be spending time with a man other than Joel for the first time in years.

Her little red post van swung into the station yard and came screeching to a halt as she almost knocked Simon flying. She certainly hadn't expected him to be outside, never mind kneeling down on the ground, folding a tarpaulin.

"We seem destined to damage one another in some way, yet I fly jumbo jets for a living and have fewer narrow escapes than when I spend two minutes in your company. Now, I'm not saying you do these things on purpose, but you do have a way of being slightly dangerous to my well-being."

Joanna pulled a face and snapped quickly back, although good-naturedly, as she found it difficult to be anything else, "Well, if you will spend time skulking around, what can you expect?"

"Skulking? I object! I am not skulking; I'm simply collecting anything that may belong to the roofers to give them no reason to come back, once I have dealt with them. If you are still able to help me, Mother says the ladder doesn't even belong to them, it's mine, so there is only this tarp to return to them."

"Yes, I'm available. I've had a word with my friends and luckily they have a few days between them on holiday and the girls are back to school on Monday, so I'm all yours until Thursday."

Joanna blushed as she realised what she had just said. She blustered on, hoping Simon hadn't noticed, saying, "I am so excited; I think I have found the loophole we have been looking for so that this nightmare with the roofers can finish once and for all."

"Come on, then, I'm sure you want to tell Mother your good news, and let's hope you're right. This is the last thing I need at the moment."

They all sat down with the coffee that Lily had prepared. She had begun to look forward so much to Joanna's morning calls. William was in his usual seat by the fire and before beginning her news Joanna went over to him. She took his hand in hers and he turned his head as she told him Holly said hello, and she would see him soon. Joanna looked for a response and felt sure there was more than a flicker in William's face as she squeezed his hand before going to sit with Simon and Lily.

"Right, well I think I have found a legal loophole that would stand up in any court. Not that I think that bunch of scoundrels would dream of taking it to court, but you never know. Anyway, there is a precedent called 'testamentary capacity', which means he or she must understand the implications of what is being signed. And, further more, the property is not William's; it belongs to Simon, you told me?"

"Yes, it does," Simon confirmed. "I own the whole station house and ticket office, which is this part where Mother and Father live."

"Oh, Joanna," Lily exclaimed, "you are brilliant! I am so grateful; *we* are so grateful, aren't we, Simon? I cannot believe I allowed myself to get into this situation, me who used to deal with legal documents every day."

Lily's voice cracked and she was visibly upset. Joanna assured her that it was nothing she could blame herself for as the type of people she was dealing with were opportunists who catch those who are at their most vulnerable.

"You have not lost all those skills you had when you worked," Joanna said. "You have simply changed one role for another, which is that of looking after William's needs."

Joanna sensed rather than saw Simon's eyes on her as she had reached to hold Lily's hand in an effort to comfort her. Leaning back to pick up her coffee cup, Joanna glanced upwards to see a strange look on Simon's face.

"Mother is right, we can never thank you enough, and it is so true that these…people…are no more than blood suckers. I also think you're right about the fact that, when we confront them with this legal loophole, they will not be able to let it drop fast enough.

"If it wasn't for the fact I want to sort things out with the property I'm looking for in the time I've taken off, which will offer a more permanent solution to Mother and Father's living arrangements, I would take great delight in taking them to court if for no other reason than to make sure they can't put some other unsuspecting elderly people through the same thing, without the good fortune of having a budding lawyer-come-postwoman as a friend."

"Hey, you have been my first case," Joanna said. "I just hope my boast is justified. We won't know until we go and confront them, so I better finish my round then pop back and collect you. Is one o'clock all right with you? Then we can go to the rental company. Do you know which one you want to go to or will the nearest one do?"

"Yes, that's fine, and I can't thank you enough for this. I'm so annoyed with myself as I cannot understand how I could have lost my licence. It stays in my wallet so how on earth it could have got lost is beyond me. And yes, one o'clock is fine and please don't hurry on my account as I won't be going anywhere."

"Well, I will be later on. I have the unenviable task of taking two eight-year-old girls for school shoes. We will have the same tactical battle as we always do but they are becoming more adept at the game than me, and they gang up against me in the shop, making me look like a real heel. In fact, crooks could take lessons from eight-year-old girls, with the faces of angels, but the tactical skills of politicians!"

Lily refused to believe it, and Joanna rolled her eyes, saying that she rested her case, before taking her leave.

Joanna hurried through the rest of her round. As she was driving back towards the station house it crossed her mind that her mundane sort of life had suddenly become, well, a bit more exciting. And, actually, she was rather enjoying the change of pace; or could it have been the thoughts of spending time with a man, who, even though she didn't want to admit it, she found she was attracted too without being able to stop herself. Pulling into the drive once again, she saw Simon closing the door behind him. He smiled, walking towards her tiny little van. She thought he looked enormous, and every bit the airline pilot, even though he wasn't in uniform now. Joanna would have loved to have seen him in that again, knowing it would have fed her uniform fetish. However, he still set her senses into overdrive with his tall figure in his navy blue wax jacket complemented by navy chinos and a cream roll-neck sweater that made his tanned skin look swarthy and quite sexy, thought Joanna. It crossed her mind that with him in the passenger seat there wouldn't be a great deal of room to change gear in her little post van.

They decided to go to the roofing address first to get that done before going to the rental company. Even though Simon did look a bit strange sitting in the passenger seat of the little van, just as Joanna had suspected, it wasn't in the least unpleasant. Joanna knew the whole area like the back of her hand so there was no need for a sat nav. She had a good idea where this company was and was not disappointed when, as they turned into a back alley, they found the rather grubby premises boasting to be roofing specialists.

Simon unfolded his long limbs climbing out of the van, and Joanna followed. She should have felt nervous about the confrontation that was to follow, as she had never been confrontational in her life. However, with Simon by her side, she felt completely safe and, armed with her newfound knowledge of the law, somehow empowered. In fact, it was for this very reason that she had taken her degree. Kevin would have been so proud as she was about to right a wrong, which had been her ambition since she was eighteen.

The insincere smiles of the man behind the desk soon disappeared when confronted by Simon who, announcing his surname and explaining his connection to Lily and William Winter, and not mincing his words, asked to see whoever called himself the 'boss'.

The man was only too pleased to excuse himself in order to get some backup in the shape of the tall man known to all as the one in charge. Joanna presumed he was the one Holly had witnessed talking to the two scruffy ones. Simon announced without any preamble who he was and his purpose in coming. He said in a cold and businesslike voice that there would be no payment of any sort and that they should think themselves very lucky that he was not pressing charges at this time, for fraud, harassment, and threatening behaviour to those who were unable to defend themselves. He added that, should there be any further attempt to defraud or further contact the Winters in any way, he would not hesitate to let the police deal with it.

The man, with an unsure, sickly grin, attempted to take back the initiative by pulling what he thought was his trump card. "I don't know what you mean, chum. I've got a contract signed by the old man to carry out all the repairs needed. It's all legal; I can show you it," he said, with a show of bravado that it was obvious he didn't quite feel.

At this, Joanna stepped forward, looking up at Simon before he could say anything about the description of William as the 'old man'. "I'm afraid, whatever 'contract' you say Mr Winter signed, is null and void for many reasons, the first being that Mr Winter is not capable of signing such a contract. Neither would it be legally binding for the very reason that Mr Winter does not have 'testamentary capacity', which means he doesn't understand the implication of what is being signed. Furthermore, the property in question does not belong to Mr Winter – it belongs to his son."

Joanna looked briefly up to where Simon was standing at her shoulder for support and the courage to go on.

"Mr Winter had a stroke three years ago and has not been able to speak, write or otherwise communicate with anyone since, so your argument that 'he signed a document' is pure fiction and I advise you to relinquish any claim whatsoever from Mr and Mrs Winter or they may feel it is worth the disruption of their lives just to see you go to prison for fraud and deception."

"What the hell?" the man sneered. "Don't give me that. Who do you think you are? A bloody postwoman and some guy I've never seen before."

Simon stepped in. "You are entitled to disbelieve what we say. However, my friend here is not simply a postwoman; she is also a fully qualified lawyer and you can take our word for it. Unless you sign now to say there will be no more contact with my parents then I will gladly go straight from here to the police, who will no doubt check the area for similar cases, which I'm in no doubt there are many."

The man huffed and muttered, telling the original occupant of the desk to give him a receipt or something, which Simon insisted he sign. He returned to his own office and slammed the door. Once they were outside in the fresh air, Joanna's face broke into a broad grin and Simon said, hardly moving his lips, to wait until they were safely in the van before cheering. As they pulled out of the back street and on to the main road, Joanna began to shake for no other reason than that she could not believe she had stood up to someone. She was really quite proud of herself even though, after the event, it was a bit scary.

She pulled into the nearest lay-by and they just burst out laughing.

"God, you were amazing, I can't believe it. Well, actually I do believe it now – you really are a lawyer. For a woman who doesn't go in for confrontation you did amazingly well."

"Ha, no, no, you had softened him up by the time I stepped in. Did you see his face when you announced who you were? Ha ha, what a laugh. I could see the wheels turning in his head trying to think of a good story about William signing the contract.

"Well, I think we can safely forget that whole nasty episode, although I do feel guilty that there are probably loads of elderly people in a similar situation with no one to speak for them. I wish that, as Alisha always says, I could be a people's advocate and stand up for those who can't do it for themselves."

It was obvious to Simon that Joanna was serious and felt really strongly about it. They talked it through again simply to enjoy and savour the pleasure of seeing the boss man's face as he was forced to climb down.

Then Joanna said, "Listen, we better get to the rental place as I must get back. I have to take the girls for shoes and I don't want to be too late."

Simon said he totally understood and suggested they should hurry as Joanna had done more than he could have hoped for.

Once at the rental company there was to be no problem hiring a car in Joanna's name.

However, it also had to be insured under her name and driven by her!

"That is, unless, of course, the Mr, Sir, is named on the lady's policy," said the woman behind the desk with a questioning look.

"Umm," sighed Simon. "This is ridiculous," he said to no one in particular.

Joanna told him, "Well, that's fine. I have my insurance documents in the van, as I am required to carry them for my job. I'll just nip out and get them while you attend to the rest of the details of the car, darling."

Simon nearly jumped out of his skin at Joanna's reference to him. His head snapped up, but just in time he realised what she was doing and replied, "No problem, darling."

Once the paperwork was signed and the car keys given for a rather nice, comfortable saloon with a fairly high octane engine, Simon and Joanna left the office after the helpful woman had pointed out their vehicle.

"There is only one slight problem," Joanna said, as soon as they were out of earshot of the woman. "How am I going to drive a car *and* a van?"

"Oh God, we're not very good at this lying business, are we? Erm, what about if I drove your van just out of the rental yard so that no one will suspect anything then we can swap over?"

"Right, okay, we simply have to get the van back to the depot, as I'm now on holiday and it will be needed next week. So you could follow me in the car; it's not far from here… Okay?"

Simon followed Joanna back to the depot, driving with particular care so that he didn't shunt into the back of her van, which would mean monumental problems. Joanna parked the van in the compound and jumped into the passenger side of the rental car with a huge sigh. They again burst out laughing.

"You know, I feel like a criminal," Joanna said, "and it's taken me years to gain my law degree. Your family are a danger to my good name and reputation."

"Well, what about me? I fly planes for a living – my reputation has to be above suspicion, and up until now I have had an impeccable record. Until some woman jumped on me in the dark, that is, and since then everything has conspired against me."

They both fell about laughing, realising they hadn't had this much fun for a long time. In fact, if feel-good feelings could be measured this was pretty high on the chart for both of them.

"Listen, I hate to be a party pooper but I must take the girls for their shoes this afternoon and time's getting on. You couldn't drop me home, could you? And we'll take the bus into town."

"Don't be ridiculous, I'll drive you in. After all, I have got your rental car. You're stuck with me for a few days until I can sort out my licence somehow. You promised, remember?"

"Well, oh yes, of course. I'll come with you wherever it is you're going, but you don't have to take me for the girls' shoes. Believe me, it's mind games from start to finish."

"No, no, I'd love to, honestly. It's all new to me so I'll see how it's done by an expert. Surely, after the way you handled the manager of the building company and the woman at the rental, how hard can it be to buy shoes for two little girls?"

"Ha, ha, don't kid yourself. These are not little girls, they are seasoned campaigners!"

Chapter 8

Simon drove expertly, as Joanna had known he would. If you can't trust an airline pilot to drive you, who can you trust? she thought. She settled the girls in the back seat of the car, introducing Simon to Precious, whom he hadn't met before and who gave him the full force of her lily white smile, which melted anyone who had a heart to mush.

"I told you," said Joanna, seeing his reaction to both little girls who looked like angels sitting in the back seat of the car, chatting with fingers and for once not speaking out loud. A dead giveaway that they wanted to discuss things in private. With Joanna's back to them she missed what they were saying, although she had a good idea on hearing their giggles coming from behind.

"You are in for a treat. You have no idea what you have let yourself in for. You probably think, how hard can it be to buy shoes for two sweet little girls? Right? Just you wait. Don't say I didn't warn you."

The first inclination of how hard it could be was after they had been into their third shop and were undecided on most of the stock. It didn't help that Simon was encouraging the girls, pulling faces behind Joanna's back when they tried on something he didn't like, or rolling his eyes with a look of approval if he liked them. However, whichever ones he liked and the girls looked hopefully at Joanna, she gave the thumbs down, saying they were not suitable for school shoes.

Eventually, Joanna promised them a McDonalds if they chose suitable, sturdy and sensible shoes. She also promised they could buy something of their choice from one of the many barrows in the mall that sold all kinds of fancy scrunchies for their hair and bits and bobs that only girls would buy. Miraculously, in the very next shop, they chose almost identical shoes as had been shown to them in the first shop.

"That also was a girl thing," said Joanna to the bemused Simon.

While the girls spent ages choosing what they were going to spend their money on at the barrows, Simon and Joanna sat down on a nearby bench. Simon noticed that, no matter how relaxed Joanna appeared to be, in her attempt to give the girls their own space in which to choose their own goodies it was still difficult for Joanna not to intervene.

Just like a mother hen, she was taking in everything that was being signed, and watching anyone who looked likely to say or do anything to upset the girls. She was also able to carry on a conversation with Simon as mothers of multiple children can.

Joanna said, "I bet you have never experienced a shopping trip like this before," laughing at his expression.

"Actually, I have really enjoyed myself."

"No, really? You are a glutton for punishment, and you are a bad influence."

"Me? How so?"

"I know you were pulling faces behind my back. I can see exactly what the girls are thinking and they would never have dared pick up such outrageous shoes if you hadn't been encouraging them."

Joanna was laughing. "I can imagine how long a pair of shoes would last if you were in charge of the shoe buying."

Simon thought for a moment about how nice it would be to take your children for shoes, and do all those things he had missed out on simply because he was never in one place long enough to form a lasting relationship with someone whom he could spend the rest of his life with and have children.

"Good grief," Joanna laughed and broke into Simon's thoughts, saying, "How long does it take to spend three pounds each? Oh, hang on, I think they have chosen. Now you must suffer the indignities of McDonalds on a Saturday afternoon. This really is the 'acid' test. If you pass this, you will get the badge of courage, given for shopping with two children for school shoes, waiting while they spend their treasured allowances on trinkets. Then subjecting your unsuspecting ears to the noise of dozens of other children, whose parents have also bribed their offspring by promising a 'happy meal'."

Joanna couldn't possibly know how much Simon was enjoying his Saturday out with what outsiders would perceive to be his family. He thought how nice it felt. He had always wondered, while sitting having a coffee in a Costa Coffee house, where very few children went as they were frowned on if they breathed out loud, what it would be like. As he watched parents with various shapes and sizes of children, he had to admit to feelings of envy. He used to wonder if that was his biological clock ticking away, and whether that was how childless women felt?

He was blasted out of his reverie by the sheer volume of sound that came as you opened the door to McDonalds. He enjoyed the simple pleasure of the girls signing so fast and speaking at the same time, saying what they wanted then changing their minds, excitedly deciding on something totally different.

After all the meals were decided, Simon insisted he went to the counter and ordered them. He carried the tray back, and the girls had all their little things they had bought from the mall on the table. They were having a show and tell for Joanna, who was attempting to make room on the table for the tray. As they ate and talked, which was a science when you needed all your fingers to talk, Joanna laughed at Simon, asking how he would sleep tonight; and betting it had been more tiring than a long-haul flight.

"Well, maybe, but take my word for it – a long-haul flight is not half so much fun as I have had today. I only wish I could sign, so I wouldn't miss most of what they are saying."

"Really? You would like to sign? It puts most people off. In fact, to be honest, they run a mile as soon as they find out that I have a child who is deaf."

Joanna looked at Simon, really looked, and she could see he really was enjoying himself and was not simply saying it as a chat-up line. Not that she really heard many chat-up lines, as most people either thought she was a married woman with a child, or knew she had a child who attended the deaf school. Straight away they were classed as 'disabled' as though that excluded them from normal society, which, she realised, was half the reason she might end up giving into Holly and allowing her to change to a 'normal hearing school' in the hope that she could integrate so well that she wouldn't be singled out as 'the deaf girl'.

The journey home was also fun. Simon would have loved to have broken into song, but that was difficult when there was only Joanna sitting in the front seat to sign what he was trying to sing. She turned it into a joke, saying he sang out of key so they were lucky they couldn't hear him. As they arrived back home at Joanna's, Simon was simply going to drop Joanna and the girls off and go. However, he knew he needed to make the arrangements for her to come with him the following day.

The girls tumbled out of the car and Joanna turned to Simon. "You are coming in for supper, aren't you? Or are you in a hurry to get back to see Lily?"

It never crossed Joanna's mind that maybe Simon didn't want to spend any more time with people he hardly knew; she could see that he had genuinely enjoyed his day.

"Oh, well, erm, we do have to make some arrangements for tomorrow and, if it's not putting you out at all, I would love to."

Reluctant for the day to end, feeling inexplicably contented at the end of a very mixed sort of day, Simon accepted and parked the car up. He followed everyone inside the front door to be met by the most delicious smell of food. Simon realised McDonalds was all right for a snack, but it was no substitute for 'food'.

The girls ran into the kitchen where the fabulous smell emanated from, and could be heard bombarding the occupants with their day.

Precious said she had got a new red scrunchie for her hair, a bracelet and some cool new school shoes.

Holly, already putting on the necklace of all different coloured beads she had bought with her money, asked Joel how she looked.

Joel, of course, said she looked, "Like a lady, my dear; and did you get cool shoes? Or hot shoes?"

Holly laughed, saying, "Cool shoes, Joel. Don't be silly, you can't buy hot shoes."

Joel waggled his eyebrows, saying, "Oh yes, you can."

The girls pushed him as they always did when he was being silly, as they called it.

Simon stood taking in the atmosphere of the happy scene, before introducing himself. "Hi, I'm Simon Winter. You must be Precious's father?"

"Hello, I am, for my sins." Joel introduced himself and put his hand out to shake Simon's. "Has she been a devil child? I don't envy you today, taking the girls for shoes. Oh my goodness, I would rather paint a ceiling than suffer the shoe day."

Simon laughed at Joel's obvious jovial character, knowing he was going to like this guy instantly. "The girls have been great, no bother whatsoever. To be honest, I haven't enjoyed a day so much in a long time."

"Oh my God, Joanna, don't let this one go. Hang on to him. Listen, by the time I've fed him he will be too full to run."

And they laughed at that because it was true that when Joel cooked he thought he was cooking for a village in the Caribbean, not a family of five.

A voice called while descending the stairs, "Is that you, Joanna? How did it go?" The voice preceded Alisha through the kitchen door.

Joel made huge eyes at her, saying accusingly, "Now who talks while not in the room?"

"Yes, but…" Then noticing they had company in the form of a gorgeous hunk of a man, or yum, yum, as the girls would say, Alisha stopped her banter with Joel and introduced herself. "Hello, I'm sorry about that, I'm Alisha. How do you do?"

Shaking Simon's hand, Alisha looked stunning as usual even in her uniform. She looked as Joel called her, a 'very handsome woman'. Simon shook hands with her and gave her one of his smiles and Joanna could tell Alisha was melting under his gaze.

Joanna rescued the situation, saying Simon had had his baptism of fire by going shopping with the girls for shoes and she exaggerated the tension. "He even took us for a McDonalds," she said with drama in her voice. This gave Alisha time to recover her blatant thoughts about Simon's obvious charms.

"Well, I hope you've left room for one of Joel's suppers or you will hurt his feelings. Then I must get to work; I'm on the late shift. So tell us what we have been waiting all day to find out. What happened with your great legal breakthrough?"

"She was like a court room lawyer." Simon joined into the spirit of the conversation.

"Oh, I was not. Simon had softened him up first with his sheer size, the fact that we had the testamentary capacity grounds, plus the facts that the property is Simon's and that poor old William could never have signed anything, as we pointed out. I think he knew when he was well beaten and dropped any further action. I must admit, Lish, it felt so good; I can't explain how good it felt to get one back for the little people. Kevin would have been proud."

At that, Joanna's voice unexpectedly cracked and she had to swallow a massive lump in her throat to recover herself. She was proud that now she was able to help those in need, something she had always aspired to even when times had appeared to conspire against her.

"Grub up, folks. Tell the girls, Lish. I am absolutely sure you will love this, simply because I am a wonderful cook, am I not, ladies?"

"Actually, we would like to contradict him, but he is the most fabulous cook. Why he didn't train to be a chef instead of a doctor, we'll never know. By now we would have had a restaurant and been rich instead of working for the NHS and making ends meet."

The girls came down and everyone was seated. The food was in serving dishes so they could eat as much or as little as they could manage, for, as usual, Joel had gone overboard and the table groaned under the weight.

"So, Simon, Joanna says you are going to start up your own business. What kind of business will that be?" Joel enquired in his easy-going manner.

Simon began to tell him that he had always wanted to set up his own freight carrying airline, but the time had never been right or it had seemed that way. Ever since his father had had his stroke and his mother was looking after him…

"Well, it's becoming increasingly obvious that I need to be there for them. I must be honest that's not the only reason," continued Simon. "I am fed up with commercial flying. It's a young man's game, never being in one place, always in a different country every other day. It's tiring and lonely if the truth were told," he said wistfully.

"Wow, I wouldn't mind swapping jobs just for a little while; I would like to experience all those things you're fed up with," said Joel.

"Poor Joel," Alisha said. "Joel seems to have been training to become a doctor ever since I first met him. It has been his dream, but the problem with dreams is they come at the expense of any other life."

"I don't regret becoming a doctor, don't get me wrong. I love my job, but Lish is right: we have never had a holiday, even a package holiday. We couldn't afford it to begin with; then we are always working and it's difficult to coordinate our days off, never mind a week."

"I don't regret being a pilot. However, there is more to flying than commercials. I would like to find a small, suitable airfield that has a house large enough for myself and maybe an annex for Mum and Dad, outbuildings, and a hangar large enough for two smaller planes. I want to haul freight as well as the courier side of things, small packages, documents, special mail, et cetera. You know the kind of thing?"

It was obvious to all that Simon was really looking forward to his new venture. Of course, to the layperson, being sick of flying off to a new destination of sea and sun must seem a lot to swallow. However, to anyone who has been alone either in life or in their work, it's not difficult to understand how it could become very lonely. Sleeping in a different hotel each night by yourself, when all those around are with friends and family and have set off to enjoy their week or two-week holiday; and it would be almost impossible to meet someone with whom you wished to have a meaningful relationship, as even most staff are usually seasonal.

No, Joanna could see why Simon longed for something more stable and fulfilling. Today she had had her first taste of what it could be like if she found a way to use the degree she had worked so hard for. The strange thing was that all the time she had studied for her future, working for the P.O. was always meant to be temporary. However, it had taken so long to gain her final degree that suddenly it was a bit scary. She knew that she would have to leave her comfort zone and do what she set out to do all those years ago when she started university, when she and Kevin were going to change things for those who were unable to.

"That will be very expensive. I mean won't you have to, pardon my ignorance, but buy planes and land and things?"

"Well, that's where Joanna comes in, if she is still willing. Don't ask me how but I have misplaced my driving licence and I'm afraid you simply can't hire a rental car without one, so we told a bit of a fib and Joanna has hired the car in her name. Unfortunately, not only can't you hire one, but you can't insure one either unless you also have said licence. So I need Joanna to take me to a couple of disused airstrips that are for sale. Actually the most expensive part are the planes. Disused airstrips aren't something everyone wants so you can often pick them up for as little as the price of a detached house with a couple of hundred acres. The problem is they are in Scotland."

Joanna's sharp intake of breath was indication that she had no idea that these little jaunts were not local.

"I could have flown but I wanted to come and see my parents. Also I'll need to drive between the two places, so driving was more of an option, if you see my meaning? The place I've researched and am most interested in is in Oban on the West of Scotland. There is a smaller one on the island of Mull; however, it does not appear to have living accommodation that is completely ready for habitation. And I must have somewhere for my parents to simply move straight into. My mum has a lot to cope with since my father's stroke. I wouldn't mind in the slightest, starting from scratch, but I would like my parents to live with me. My intension is some sort of shared accommodation, not unlike what we have at the moment, so that I spend more time with them but we both have our independence."

The girls, who had been watching the conversation, asked excitedly if they could go up in a plane when Simon bought one, as though this was something you did every day, like giving someone a lift.

"I'll take both of you up in one of my planes and that's a promise."

The girls squealed in delight, almost deafening everyone else. The girls were excused and Alisha said she must be making tracks or she would be late. Alisha gave Joanna a look that said 'You must tell me all when you get back'. Joanna took the opportunity to suggest Simon fill her in on his plans before it got too late.

Joel started to clear the table, giving them room to have coffee and make plans. Looking every bit the part, in his man-size apron declaring that he was the best chef in the world, he liked to clear and wash the dishes himself, so Joanna didn't feel in the least guilty that he had also made the supper, which had actually been one of her favourites – Cajun jambalaya, with Hawaiian rice salad, and caramelised pineapple and bananas?

As Joel washed the dishes, they all chatted over coffee deciding on the best route to take to get to Oban, then on to Mull, which would involve getting the ferry across. Joel said surely they would have to stay one or even two nights as they couldn't possible see everything in such a short time. Simon didn't like to take advantage of Joanna, he said, knowing she had Holly to look after.

"Oh, don't you be worrying about Holly. We'll look after Holly, and I am having a few days off and the girls are at school during the day. Just you be having a little break, Joanna, you deserve it. She never goes anywhere, and you're always covering for us, so just you go tomorrow and get an early start girl. Go, go, I tell you."

"The 'man of the house' has spoken," said Joanna, with pretended reverence in her tone. "Actually, Joel's probably right. We should make an early start tomorrow just in case it takes a day or two to see both sites."

"Are you sure? It's very good of you, Joanna. Really, I don't know how to thank you."

"Oh, you don't say that to a woman, man. The next thing you know they will have thought of a way." Joel's great belly laugh was contagious and Joanna threatened to tell Alisha, to which Joel pretended to cower, begging her not to do that in a grovelling voice.

"I really can't thank you enough, Joanna, and I know Mum will be so relieved that she doesn't have to worry about roofers and other problems that she can well do without." Simon sounded relieved.

"Honestly, you don't have to thank me. I really enjoy feeling useful, and it gives me something to think about for the future."

Shortly after, Joanna climbed into the driver's side, adjusted the seat to her leg length, and drove the short journey to the old station, which would give her a chance to get the hang of the car for the drive home on her own.

"I can't remember the last time I had such an enjoyable day," Simon said."I mean that. I have thoroughly enjoyed every bit of it, right down to the McDonalds with the girls, and being included in the family meal, and for your invaluable help sorting out Mum and Dad's problem."

Joanna shrugged off his thanks, saying she would collect him at nine a.m. and that she would call in and see Lily and William for a minute before they left. A quick wave and a flash of her lights and she was off.

Chapter 9

Driving home in the darkness gave Joanna a chance to process the day. One of the things she enjoyed about her job was the time she spent driving around in her van. She used to often say how she had some of her best ideas while driving from A to B. Today had been a strange sort of day, she thought. It had started off a bit scary, having to actually face up to tradesmen who appeared to have the power of…well, damn right gall and audacity, she knew that. But, somehow, those sort of people made a person feel that they would win any kind of argument. You were left feeling you would rather back down simply to be rid of them.

For the first time in Joanna's life, since Kevin and she were at university and were going to change the world, she felt as though she had at last begun on the route to a proper career. A journey that had started all those years ago, before she had found she was pregnant with Holly. Alone and with no one to turn to once Kevin had gone, Joanna had thought she would end up just as her own mother had, becoming a single parent and ruining any chance of a future for herself or her child.

Today, she had proved to herself that she was not like her mother, and that, although she had taken an unconventional route, she had made it at last. Pride swelled inside Joanna and brought tears to her eyes as she drove along in the darkness. The sheer enormity of what she had achieved began to dawn on her, and into the bargain she had a wonderful child. How great is that? thought Joanna.

She knew that very soon she must come to a decision about her work at the Post Office and her ambition to use her newly acquired skills to help others like Lily and William, people who didn't know where to turn when their problems seemed insurmountable. Joanna wanted to be there for people like them, now more than ever before.

And then there was Simon. Wow, thought Joanna, letting her brain talk freely while there was only her listening, She thought to herself, hmm, rather nice, and for the first time in a long time she thought about what it must be like having a partner. She remembered only too well the odd couple of dates she had attempted since having Holly. There were a few well-meaning people at work who would set her up with a date. They usually consisted of a drink after work or a movie, but once they found out she had a child, then even worse that the child was deaf, they ran like a hare on steroids into the distance.

To be honest, thought Joanna, up until now... Well... Yes, she answered her brain, yes, until Simon, she hadn't really given it a thought. Now she had met Simon, though, and enjoyed his company, it might be nice to be part of a twosome for a change.

Whatever happens is fine, she thought, and probably nothing will. After all, she was just helping him until his licence was sorted out. He would probably be horrified if he knew she was even contemplating anything more than that. But in the meantime, she repeated to her brain, she was looking forward to her trip away. She knew that Holly would be fine and she hadn't had a day away for, oh, years, so she intended to enjoy every minute.

On arriving back home Joanna parked the car in the drive gingerly as it was much larger than she was used to. She went straight upstairs as she wanted to catch Holly before she went to sleep. Holly, bless her, must have been waiting for her, because normally she would have been fast asleep. Joanna knew there would be little time in the morning to speak properly as mornings were frantic in their household.

Joanna entered Holly's bedroom, which was lit by the lamp on the side table. She sat on the end of her bed as she so often did at night when they would have their private chats about their days.

"Hey, we had a good day, didn't we?"

Holly signed and said that the day had been brill, and wasn't Simon great, and wasn't he handsome? Didn't Joanna think so?

"Woah, yes, the day was very enjoyable, and I must say I was very impressed with your and Precious's manners. Simon thought you were both angels, but don't worry I put him straight. I told him you both belong to the devil. Ha ha, only kidding. He had a wonderful time and he enjoyed you girls' company. He said he even enjoyed the McDonalds. Now that's a brave man.

"Listen, are you okay about me going away for a few days with Simon? We are just going to look at some disused airfields. I hadn't actually realised they were in Scotland, mind, but I will enjoy the break. Are you okay with this?"

"Mum, go, enjoy. I am nearly nine, you know, and I am perfectly safe with Joel and Alisha. I want you to have a nice time with Simon. Mum, if Joel says it's all right, will it be all right if we call and see William and Lily? I want to make sure William is all right, can I? He might have missed me. He may not know why I haven't been to see him, you see, because I'm back at school, and I would like Precious to meet him. Would that be all right with you?"

Just before Joanna stood up to leave, Holly signed, "Oh, and Mum, have a lovely time with Simon." Holly said this with a cheesy grin on her face Joanna knew meant that she would tell Precious every word and that they would discuss what they hoped would happen. Something from a television soap, no doubt.

"Okay, if you're sure about everything? I will ring Joel or Alisha and keep you up to date on what's happening and when I'll be back, okay?"

Joanna kissed Holly and gave her a hug before putting out the light.

She thought she had better think about packing a few clothes, then pondered that she had better make them warm clothes as it was probably going to be arctic conditions. She thought she had better nip downstairs and ask Joel if she could borrow his small holdall.

"Small holdall? I have never known a woman yet who could take a small bag away with her. You should see them when they arrive in the hospital for a two-day operation – you would think they were going abroad. Their cases are so large they won't fit into the lockers.

"Take it, take it. We never get a chance to go away – these bags haven't been used since our honeymoon. The middle one is probably the one you should take, though, because it will be bitter cold, brrr. You will need to take very warm clothes. If I were going I would take a balaclava – I can't stand the cold."

"I know, Joel, you hate the cold, it's your West Indian blood, but can you just imagine how fetching I would look in a balaclava, two coats, jeans and boots, which is what you would have me wearing? I am a great deal tougher than you are; I am accustomed to the cold, being a postwoman, remember? I'm going to take a glass of wine upstairs. Would you like one? Then I'm off to pack my thermals and have a long bath."

Joanna decided two pairs of trousers were more than enough. One was a pair of black cords that she had bought recently and were almost new as she had hardly had a chance to wear them. She would travel in her newest denim jeans, cream polo-neck sweater and her navy body warmer with her heavy quilted puffer-type jacket on the back seat for when she got out. She thought she had better take a smart pair of trousers, too, so she packed grey ones that she usually teamed up with a knitted vest top and a little wool biker jacket. She'd bought this outfit for last year's staff outing, which had been the only time she had ever worn it. Finally, as an extra, just in case she really was cold, she threw in a soft pink cowl-neck sweater.

She would wear her ankle boots, which were sturdy and waterproof. Surely she wouldn't need anything else, she thought. It felt very strange, packing to go somewhere. She didn't think she had ever actually done it before; she was going to have widen her horizons. Not that she wanted to travel, as such, but never having been away was a bit ridiculous at her age.

She went to have a quick word with Joel and Alisha, who were lounging on the sofa together since Alisha had got in from work, complaining that her feet hurt. Alisha tapped the seat beside her so that Joanna would come and have a chat before going to bed. Alisha wanted to know all the gossip, she said.

"Alisha, you are as bad as the girls. There is only Joel who has not hinted at any innuendo between Simon and me."

"Well, I don't need to because my woman and my daughter will get to know everything and tell me all," Joel said, waggling his eyebrows suggestively.

"There is nothing going on between Simon and me. We are going to find a suitable airfield for his new business. He is not looking for a wife and, as far as I am concerned, I am not looking for a husband."

"Rubbish," said Alisha. "I saw you peeking at him while he was talking with the girls. Woman, now, don't deny it," said Alisha.

"No, I don't. Well, I, yes, I was looking, simply because I was so interested that he apparently not only enjoyed the girls' company, but it didn't seem to bother him that they spoke in sign. He really didn't seem to mind. I was simply intrigued to see a man who didn't run a mile when seeing two deaf people talk to each other. You know what I mean?"

Alisha and Joel nodded, knowing all too well what Joanna meant. "Although," said Alisha, shoving Joel in the ribs and speaking in a stage whisper, "Joanna definitely noticed what a handsome man Simon was. Don't let her fool you – a woman knows, you know." She giggled.

Joanna remonstrated, "It's worse than being a teenager in this house! I have to account to not only my own daughter but yours as well and then you two matchmakers. Anyway, I'm off to bed as I am picking Simon up at nine-ish. I'll have my phone so I can keep in touch with you all."

With that Joanna went up to bed, Alisha and Joel giggling in the background, saying, "Mmm," suggestively. She called down the stairs good-naturedly to them that she denied everything and that they had to mind their own business.

Joanna thought to herself that she must get to sleep and stop thinking too much; she was like a schoolgirl going on a trip. She told herself to get a grip or she would be no good tomorrow, before eventually drifting off to sleep.

Chapter 10

Joanna couldn't deny she was really looking forward to her trip away, as normally when she had a few days' holiday it was to catch up on housework or gardening. She had never actually had a trip away since having Holly, so her tummy was doing somersaults. Joanna denied even to herself that it had anything to do with the fact that she was going with Simon.

She waved the girls off with Joel and had a last-minute look to make sure she had everything she needed. Then she sat reluctantly down to have another cup of coffee, which she really didn't want but would stop her from turning up too early to pick Simon up. She had been up and dressed since quarter to seven, which to Joanna was a lie-in; but, once dressed, she had found it almost impossible to sit still. Alisha was still asleep after her long shift the evening before, and Joanna tried not to make any noise. In the end she couldn't wait any longer and decided she would simply drive slowly. If she arrived too early she would spend the time with William and Lily, who were up at the crack of dawn under normal circumstances.

The sun shone warmly on a perfect autumnal morning. The leaves, already golden, were beginning to fall into the gutters, heralding the approach of winter. Joanna pulled into the station yard in the shiny rental car. As she approached the door Lily opened it as normal. Joanna knew by now that Lily had a chair at the window where she watched the world go by and that's how she knew when she was approaching. It was almost her only contact with the outside world now that William was housebound.

"Morning, Lily, how are you and William? Isn't it a beautiful day?"

Lily leant forward and hugged Joanna, which actually took Joanna by surprise.

"I have wanted to thank you for what you have done for William and me. I can't thank you enough for all your help. Simon told us what happened and that you were superb. He said you threw the legal book at them and they backed down immediately."

Joanna laughed, saying she thought Simon was being too generous and that she didn't think they would have surrendered quite so easily if it hadn't been for the fact that she had a great hulking man with her.

"I think they thought that this one simply wasn't worth the fight. I honestly think that if more people had someone to speak for them and didn't simply roll over and pay, then those types of business would soon move on or die a death. I feel for those who have no relatives or anyone to speak for them. Oh, listen to me: I'm off again on my soap box."

As they reached the lounge and Joanna saw William sitting in his usual chair she went over to say hello and to tell him that Holly was going to come and see him in a day or two. "She has asked me to tell you not to forget she is coming, all right?" said Joanna, and touched his hand.

Just then Simon came through with his overnight bag, saying to Joanna that she was an early bird and he hoped he hadn't kept her waiting. Joanna gulped hard as she took in his sheer presence. God, she must be starved of male companionship because she had to drag her eyes away from his masculine bulk and the smell. Oh my goodness, what on earth was that gorgeous smell? Some very expensive body spray, she presumed, from some foreign country.

"No, no, really, I am simply an early riser. Years of practice, I suppose, being a postwoman."

They said their goodbyes to William and Lily, and Simon pulled the car out of the station yard and their journey had started. Joanna thought she would find it impossible to be any more excited if she were going on a plane for the first time. She chided herself, deciding that she must in future do more with her and Holly's time off. Otherwise, Holly would end up never going anywhere or mixing with anyone other than those who were also deaf.

Joanna suddenly realised the irony of her thoughts, for wasn't that exactly what Holly had been banging on about? Why she wanted to go to a mainstream school next year? Joanna made the decision that when she got home she would tell Holly she could change schools next year. She would start to widen both her and Holly's horizons as she didn't want Holly living a solitary life afraid to try new things simply because she was deaf. Hundreds of famous people achieved many things despite their disability.

"You're very quiet; you don't mind this trip, do you? I realise it's a bit of a huge ask for someone you hardly know."

"No, no, I'm fine, to be honest."

Joanna suddenly decided to let him in on the fact that this was her first trip away ever and that she hadn't realised how unfair she had been to Holly to deny her the excitement she was feeling at this moment.

"I feel as though I have made a career of 'bringing up Holly', coping with our day-to-day lives. Joel was right in what he said; that we have been so busy with our heads down looking after our jobs, our children and our house that none of us has taken any time out to enjoy life."

"But you do enjoy your life, I've witnessed it. You are so happy, all of you. Your girls are so well adjusted considering their…"

"Disability. Don't be afraid to say it. The problem is, I am beginning to wonder if we haven't collectively been holding ourselves back because we were afraid to let go. Do you know what I mean? Joel and Alisha weren't kidding when they said they had never been back to visit relatives and they have lots back in Barbados. They have been so busy working and doing what's best for Precious, they never do anything for themselves."

"And you, Joanna, what do you do for yourself, apart from take on battles for people you hardly know?"

"Well, to be honest, I am just as guilty as Joel and Alisha. We seem to have made a career out of bringing up our children who happen to be deaf. Don't get me wrong – that was in itself a massive undertaking. No one can prepare you for the shock of finding out that a simple little thing like having no hearing is going to close so many doors to you and your child.

"When I first found out Holly was deaf, I thought my biggest problem was leaving university and finding a job. When I found a job with the Post Office, they were brilliant. They gave her a place in the crèche and allowed me flexi working conditions. I couldn't have asked for better friends and colleagues. But it soon became obvious that, although she was safe at the crèche, she wasn't able to join in the things that other toddlers were doing. She wasn't able to talk or communicate because she didn't know how, so I had to make the decision to move away from Leeds. I knew I had to find a school for the deaf who would take a child as young as three. Not only that, I had to hope that I could get a transfer or find another job.

"Again, the Post Office were fantastic. When I told them the school I hoped to get her into was in Derby, they arranged a transfer for me. The rest is history, so to speak – she went to the nursery attached until she was old enough to go to the school proper."

"And how did you meet Joel and Alisha?"

"Oh, well, that was a stroke of amazing good luck. They were in the same position as me. Precious was also three and they had researched and also found the only school for the deaf that took children as young as three into the nursery. They made the bold move to relocate to the Royal Derby Hospital. We met at the B & B where we were both staying in order that we could be interviewed by the school."

"Interviewed?" queried Simon. "By a school? I've never heard of such a thing. As if you didn't have enough to worry about…" he said with real concern in his voice.

"Oh yes, places at the school, especially nursery places that start at three years old, are really sought after. The thing is, it was becoming obvious by the age of three that if Holly didn't learn to sign she would never learn to talk, and, although at first I just wanted to shut out the world and keep her safe, I knew that would be unfair to Holly. Joel and Alisha had come to the same conclusion by the time Precious was three and that's how Holly and Precious are the same age."

"And you chose to live together?"

"Well, when we started to talk to each other, explaining that we all needed to work and would need child care as neither of us wanted our children to board, we knew that neither of us could afford child care as well as other expenses, but if we pooled our resources maybe we could help each other. And that's what we did and we have been so lucky because we all get on so well. We are like family."

"And now, if we are sharing our life histories, what's yours? How did you become a pilot?"

Simon took a deep breath and said that his history was a little boring in comparison to Joanna's.

"I'm thirty-seven, was married, now widowed [this was said quickly so no questions were invited on the subject]. I was in the RAF for ten years before leaving to fly commercial airlines. I am now ready for a change. You could say I'm going through a mid-life crisis. I feel that, if I don't do it now, the dream I had while serving in the RAF, of having my own planes and running a cargo-come-courier service, will never happen.

"And there's Mum and Dad. I feel so guilty when things happen, such as the roof episode, and I'm not there so Mum has to cope on her own. It's hard enough for her since Dad took ill. He used to be a solicitor, you know, and a good one by all accounts. Mum was his secretary when they married. And look at him now – that's not the father I remember. He was a busy, intelligent, kind, caring guy. Then, suddenly, this inexplicable illness. It's as though he has simply shut down.

"I just think they did everything for me. They supported me when I needed them and now it's my turn to support them, so one of my priorities when looking at the airfield is also the accommodation, which must be either large enough to convert or suitable for us all to move into. I wouldn't mind doing 'some' alterations; however, I need it to be habitable for their sake.

"The station house has been ideal because I have my privacy in the main house and they have theirs in the ticket house, but I worry when I'm not home, and, to be honest, this has given me the push I needed. So let's hope we see something that suits all our purposes."

"It sounds so exciting," Joanna said, "starting a new life. Oh, I hadn't realised how far we have travelled. Such wonderful scenery. I am excited for you."

"Would you like to stop for a while or push on?" Simon asked. "We can stop at Carter Bar, which is where the English and Scottish borders cross."

"Oh, that sounds wonderful. We will stop there, and I will be able to say I am in Scotland."

Simon laughed, saying she was easily pleased. He was used to seasoned travellers on commercial flights complaining about the food and drink and the lack of leg room. They drove through the most magnificent scenery and Joanna was absorbed in how beautiful the hills were. Simon explained that they were the Cheviot Hills, which seemed to cloak the valleys below. Joanna thought how knowledgeable he was and had to stop herself from starting her own campaign of hero worship towards her first male companion.

They soon arrived at Carter Bar and Joanna was absolutely fascinated with the signposts on either side declaring England on one side and Scotland on the other, but the best of all was that she could hear bagpipe music. "Can you?" she asked Simon. As they climbed out of the car in order to stretch their legs Simon pointed to where the music was coming from. And to Joanna's delight, standing on a stone plinth, was a piper in full Scottish regalia playing 'Flower of Scotland'. Joanna was beside herself to get close enough to take a photograph on her phone so that she could show Holly when she got home.

"I thought he may be here but as it's the end of the summer season I wasn't sure he would be, so I didn't tell you before because I didn't want to disappoint you."

Seeing the obvious delight on Joanna's face made Simon think how much Holly and Precious would have loved the sight. Even if they couldn't enjoy the music as he and Joanna did, seeing a man in a kilt would be something different.

They eventually moved on and into Jedburgh where they stopped for lunch at a small café, eating in companionable silence. Simon was enjoying watching Joanna's obvious enjoyment at all things new, and Joanna was enjoying the way other diners would assume that she and Simon were a couple. How sad is that? thought Joanna, but nothing was going to depress her, today of all days. Other diners probably thought what a handsome couple they made, her with her wonderful thick, wavy, blonde hair and eyes bright with excitement, and him so dark and Celtic looking, and both obviously happy and enjoying each other's company.

When they were fed and watered and were back on the road again, Simon said to Joanna, "When you were at university, you mentioned a Kevin… Was he Holly's father?"

"Yes, Kevin and I met at university and we were together for two years until the accident."

Joanna seemed to be remembering, trawling back through her thoughts, when she slowly continued, "Yes, Kevin was my boyfriend. We were going to change the world. He was adopted as a child, by a couple who should never have stayed together. They were unhappy and thought adopting a child would make things better. Instead, all it meant for Kevin was an unhappy life, with unhappy parents who let him know that as soon as he left to go to university they would part. Knowing he wasn't wanted or even particularly liked made Kevin desperate to find out who and why his birth mother gave him up for adoption. He was always doing research in an attempt to find her, and it wasn't until after his death that I found the address and made contact."

"Listen, you needn't talk about this if it's too painful," Simon told her. "I totally understand and respect your privacy."

"No, actually I hadn't realised how good it would feel to get it out in the open. Joel and Alisha know, but generally I have put it to the back of my mind and never refer to it.

"Kevin was a great one for demonstrations and he was always going to right every wrong, fight for all the little people. That's how I know Kevin would have got so much enjoyment out of getting one over on the roofing company.

"Well, we set out on the demonstration from our halls of residence, in our woolly hats and painted faces with some slogan or other. To tell you the truth, I can't even remember what we were demonstrating against at the time.

"But we marched and chanted and in the throng, being pushed, pulled and generally dragged along, we sang and generally made a nuisance of ourselves until the police arrived to move us on. There was the usual scuffling and shoving and as we surged forward we lost touch. By the time I got to a place where I could stand on a wall and look for him through the mêlée all I saw was a pile of woolly clothing lying on the ground with a brightly coloured bobble hat on. It was one I had knitted for him – it was horrible but he wore it because I had made it for him specially.

"There was no big mystery, no foul play, he had simply slipped in the scuffle and cracked his head on the pavement. The hospital said he had a thin skull and that it could have happened at any time in his life. Well, it happened during one of his many demonstrations that he enjoyed more than anything, and while he was young and vital, full of spirit. The one thing I regret is that he never knew that I was pregnant. Well, neither did I at that time."

Joanna had become thoughtful and almost silent, until her voice regained its strength, saying that a lot of good had come out of Kevin's search for his birth mother. It turned out that she wasn't like her own mother, a druggy who had given her child up. Kevin's parents were both profoundly deaf and had been forced to give him up. The authorities had said they must as they were 'disabled' and could not care for a child. They made him a ward of court and simply took him.

Joanna continued, saying that when she found the address among Kevin's personal effects, which his adopted parents didn't even bother coming to collect, she took Holly, who was a baby at that time, to meet them, to tell them that they had a grandchild.

"You can't imagine the shock of finding out that they were both deaf. It answered so many questions for me. I had no medical history, as I was brought up with lots of different foster parents and there was very little of my history documented other than the fact that my mother was an alcoholic and a druggy who gave her baby up. So to find Kevin had real parents who had a history to tell was wonderful.

"They are such lovely people; and they were the only people who offered me help when I was at my wits' end. They offered me a roof over my head, but I knew that wasn't the answer. However, they often used to send me little packages with baby clothes in and a ten pound note pushed inside. We don't get to see them very often as it is so hard to communicate with them. They don't sign very well and, to be honest, I never seem to have the time to do more than send a card or make a quick visit if I'm over that way in the van."

Joanna took a deep breath and brought herself down to earth, saying, "Gosh, it's amazing what a long journey will make you reveal about yourself! I hope I haven't bored you to death with my woes. I have a wonderful life and wouldn't change a thing about my past so don't get me wrong and don't feel sorry for me."

"You certainly haven't bored me. I have been totally fascinated by your interesting life and how you have battled on through adversity to become such a…"

"Oh no, no, I haven't battled on; I have been blessed, and I had the pleasure of knowing Kevin, having Holly. I have recently told myself, after our victory over the villains, that, although I have done things the long way round, I have got there in the end. So don't feel sorry for me, as I am ready to start my life now. You have made my mind up, and I must lift my head out of the sand and move on, for Holly's sake if not for my own."

"So we are both looking for a new start."

"Yes, I think we are. It's a bit scary, isn't it?"

Chapter 11

By the time they arrived in Oban darkness had fallen. However, you couldn't mistake the lights from the harbour along which was strung a row of brightly lit shops and restaurants; and, of course, the ferry terminal was a hive of industry.

Simon suggested the first thing they should do was book into a hotel. They found a nice hotel right on the front near the harbour and ferry terminal, which would be suitable when they went to see the second of the two airstrips that Simon wanted to see. Tomorrow they would concentrate on the one just outside Oban and the following day they would take the ferry across to Mull.

As Simon approached the desk to book their rooms, Joanna stood slightly behind. When he requested two single rooms, the woman behind the desk glanced up in surprise. That wasn't what she was expecting, thought Joanna, and glanced away so that the woman couldn't read her expression.

The receptionist directed them to the top floor and told them it was the two rooms at the front facing the harbour. Joanna was glad as she was so looking forward to seeing the comings and goings of the harbour. Simon opened her door, having a glance inside to make sure it was up to his standard, then gave Joanna her key and went to his own door. They agreed that they would go downstairs for supper as soon as they had unpacked.

Joanna barely had time to unpack her things after spending time mesmerised at the view from her window, which to her delight was a bay window with a seat, just right for sitting for hours gazing at the ferries and the island in the distance, which she had been told was the isle of Mull.

"Hey, you decent?" shouted Simon as he began to open the door.

"Yes, come in. I'm sorry, I've been distracted by watching all the goings-on in the harbour. Is that the Isle of Mull over there?"

"Yes, we will look at the Oban site tomorrow and then on Tuesday we can get the ferry over to Mull and take a look at the other one, if that suits? I have my reservations about the one at Mull, but as it's on my shortlist I intend to see it. Are you hungry? I think I could eat a horse and something smells nice. If you're ready, we'll go down?"

Joanna was glad she had at least brushed her teeth and run a comb through her hair. A quick squirt of perfume and that was all she had time for. She guessed the same could be said of Simon. She also guessed that he must be very hungry.

The dining room overlooked the harbour and Joanna thought how wonderful it all was. She couldn't have been having a better time. She had to pinch herself to make sure she wasn't in bed with her alarm going off at five thirty for work.

"Hey, you've gone all quiet on me again," said Simon. "Are you tired after the journey? I was going to suggest a walk around the harbour when we have eaten, but if you are too tired just say and I'll understand."

"Oh no, to be honest, I'm pinching myself to make sure this isn't all a dream. Two weeks ago I was delivering mail and I hardly knew who you were and now I'm on holiday with you in this wonderful place.

"Oh, I know to you this isn't a holiday. You being such a traveller going all over the world, this must seem pretty provincial. But to me this is somewhere I had no idea I would ever be. It may only be Scotland, but I couldn't have chosen a nicer place. I am mentally promising myself to bring Holly here for a holiday one day."

Simon smiled at Joanna's innocence – not only that she had never been anywhere but that she would tell him. Most girls would bluff their way along, pretending that they had seen it all. Something about Joanna's innocence made everything more exciting for him. It gave him pleasure to show Joanna sights for the first time that he had seen many times.

When their meal was finished they collected their warm coats as the evening had become quite chilly. However, that would not deter them from a bracing walk along the harbour.

As they walked and talked, Joanna decided to take her chance and ask about his wife.

"Stop me if you don't want to talk about it, or if it hurts too much, but you mentioned you had been married and were now widowed?"

There was a small silence then Simon started slowly, saying yes he had been married, but it had all been over so quickly he wondered if he had ever really been a married man.

"But yes, we were married for two years, and she died. She died of ovarian cancer. She was a pilot," he went on. "We met in the RAF, and fell in love, which was frowned upon so we kept it secret. Then, when we thought she was pregnant, we were going to have to let the cat out of the bag. However," he went on slowly, "it wasn't a baby, it was cancer; and by the time she knew it was too late."

"Oh, Simon, how terrible."

"Can't be helped, it's one of those things. You don't think so at the time but, like you, life goes on. And you know the rest. I never felt happy in the force after that so it wasn't long before I left to go to commercial stuff. And now here I am ready to start a new chapter."

Simon saw a shiver run down Joanna's spine and pulled her towards him, putting his arm around her to keep her warm, telling her if she wanted to go back, just to say. Joanna quickly assured him she was enjoying the night air and was fine now. However, Simon didn't remove his arm and Joanna felt a warm glow from deep within her.

After walking around the town as the streets began to empty, they decided they would make their way back and have a nightcap in the bar before going to bed.

Joanna thought she had such a lot to dream about it would be almost impossible to get any sleep tonight.

As they climbed the stairs towards their rooms, Simon resumed his arm around her, and Joanna couldn't remember feeling so happy. She scolded herself for simply forgetting to live, and saw that she hadn't realised she had allowed her sensible head to take over her life. Where had the Joanna gone who went on demonstrations, painted her face, sang and chanted with other mad students…? She had grown up. She had had to grow up very fast. That's where she'd gone: she was a mother, a bread winner…

"Hey, you've gone quiet again. You okay?"

"Yes, yes, I'm more than okay. I'm very okay," Joanna said in a happy, dreamy sort of voice.

Simon, who had got used to having his arm around Joanna's shoulders and had enjoyed the feeling, let it drop to his side as they walked up the corridor. However, it had created closeness where previously they had been separate, two people sharing a journey. As they reached their respective doors Simon reached out, placing a hand on either side of Joanna's large puffer jacket. She could feel the warmth from his fingers. Simon looked down with a wry smile on his face and gave her a fleeting kiss, which was over almost before it had begun.

"Goodnight, Joanna Berry. You have no idea how appealing you are at this precise moment."

With that cryptic sentiment he gently pushed her into her room, closing the door behind her. Joanna stood in the same spot with her eyes closed, attempting to relive the last few minutes in order to feel again that fleeting kiss. She put her fingers to her lips as though they would reveal some secret. Her insides had shot up into her throat with a feeling she hardly recognised, and that she had thought was dead.

It was obvious to Joanna that her life had changed from the minute this journey had begun; the scales had dropped from her eyes.

In her struggle to survive she realised that she had left life behind, and, although there was nothing wrong with how she had achieved her goal, which had been to give Holly the best start in life she could, and to finish her university dream, somehow on the way she had forgotten how to live life and Holly had begun to notice. Such a young child; yet she saw what Joanna hadn't, that there was more to life than what came out of the protected environment in which they had cocooned themselves.

Joanna sat staring out to sea from the window seat with the duvet wrapped around her, content to sit all night. However, common sense told her she must attempt to sleep, even though her mind was in turmoil, a mixture of unadulterated happiness and a degree of reminiscence.

Joanna woke bright and early the next day, which was usual for her. Today was different from her normal day of collecting the mail, though, she thought. Today she was staying in a hotel, with a fabulous view, with a gorgeous male of a different kind. She found it almost impossible to contain her excitement. How much pleasure could one person get without sex being involved...? Joanna's face burned red, with feelings of guilt. After her fleeting kiss from Simon the night before, her mind had begun to stray into the murky memories of her limited sexual experience. It was something that she had locked away since the birth of her child, but from which a flame had begun to rekindle, a flame that Joanna had no intentions of snuffing out.

A knock at her door made her jump out of her personal reverie. She had been dressed for ages so, having no last-minute changes to make to her appearance, she opened the door, her heart pounding with the excitement of seeing Simon and starting another wonderful day together, full of new experiences.

"Morning, did you sleep okay?" said Simon, looking freshly showered and smelling good enough to eat, thought Joanna. If she hadn't slept it was all his fault, she thought, but she wouldn't change it for the world.

"Yes, yes, I had a wonderful night. I've been up ages but I can't take my eyes off the view. To think I have lived in a town surrounded with other houses all my life and I never realised what I was missing out on. I would give anything to live near the sea, and Holly would absolutely love it."

"You ready for today? I am really excited myself; I hope that the base is as good as it looks on the Internet. This could be the one, the place we up and move to lock, stock and barrel – my dream."

Joanna experienced a tinge of sadness when Simon referred to moving, but she was determined to enjoy every day and everything about this trip, so pushed any thoughts of never seeing Simon again to the back of her mind.

They had a wonderful breakfast that would keep them going all day. Joanna was not really a breakfast person but the smell was so delicious she had succumbed to the temptation and thoroughly enjoyed it.

Simon checked the map before they set out to find the disused airstrip, which should be pretty easy to spot, especially as the advert said it still had the control tower intact.

As they drove along the country roads, Joanna's thoughts turned to being surrounded by sea, yet wonderful countryside seemed such a bonus. Downright greedy, she thought, to those of us who see mostly houses. Although she did live in a beautiful area of Derbyshire, and the Peak District was without doubt beautiful, she hadn't realised that to be beside the sea gave you a feeling of such freedom – to be able to look as far as the eye could see and there be no end to it.

They hadn't been on the road more than fifteen minutes when they saw the first indication that they were indeed on the right route. They could see the tower in the distance, sitting on the flat runways that crisscrossed the field. In the distance they could see a huge hangar, which Simon knew would be much larger as they got closer. They followed the signs that took them down a lane, suddenly coming to two large stone pillars with a large gate that Joanna said she would jump out and open provided it wasn't padlocked.

Driving through the gate and up a very long tarmac road-come-drive, the first building they came to was a rather large stone-built house, with a porch at the front and four square windows, one in each corner, making it look rather like a doll's house. It was a nice house, thought Joanna, friendly but a bit neglected. It needed a Virginia creeper or roses around the porch. As she looked at the house, Simon was obviously looking farther on towards the business side of the property. Typical, she thought: women want to nest and men want to explore.

As they bypassed the house in order to find the hangars and see the actual land and the condition of the runways, Joanna turned to look over her shoulder back towards the stone dwelling. Simon saw her whimsical look, even though his mind was on the outbuildings, size and quantity. He said for her not to worry as there was supposed to be some keys left in one of the outbuildings and she would get a really good mooch around the house soon.

"Oh, great, I love to look round empty properties. I love to imagine they are mine and how I would alter them."

"Ha, typical woman. I have never met a woman yet who could simply move in and love it. They even change hotel rooms, can you believe?"

"Ha, you sound like Joel. He thinks we are a different species, from Mars, he says. And you are right: women like to make their mark, make it their home and not someone else's."

Simon parked up outside the larger of the two hangars, which did indeed look enormous close up.

"How many planes would you get in there, for goodness sake?"

"Oh, well, it would certainly fit the two that I intend to purchase, with room for expansion in the future. It's in remarkable condition from what I can see. It's hard to imagine that this hangar has been here for God knows how many years. One thing about buying ex RAF buildings – they were built to last and were kept in regular order. Everything was maintained constantly.

"This is looking really good to me. The runway looks in amazingly good condition, considering it hasn't been used for ages. I do know that a small company used the runway and the hangar for a short time, but other than that it's been here since its RAF days."

They spent a good two hours walking the length and breadth of the airfield and in and out of all the outbuildings, which needed very little repairs if any, thought Simon. As they climbed back into the car Simon noticed that Joanna looked almost blue with the cold, and put the heater full on.

"You should have told me you were cold; you look perished. I'm afraid I got carried away. You should have said."

"No, no, honestly, I'm fine, really. What's a bit of cold when you are enjoying yourself?"

"Enjoying yourself? I'm sorry; I forget this is probably not as exciting to you as it is to me."

"No, really, Simon, don't even think about it. I really am enjoying every bit of it, and you are just like a woman. I could see you practically moving all your stuff in, as women do when they see a house. Speaking of houses, did you find any keys so that we can have a look inside?"

"No. I'm presuming they mustn't have any vandal problems here as all the outbuildings and hangars were left unlocked, so I'm hoping the house is open as well."

As they pulled up in front of the house again, Joanna couldn't wait to find out if it was open. She would be so disappointed if it wasn't. Simon tried the door, but it was definitely locked, and Joanna's face dropped. However, after Simon bent down to a flower pot outside the front door, he triumphantly lifted the key to show Joanna she could get out of the car.

Warmed through and ready to explore, Joanna leapt out of the car reinvigorated. Simon had unlocked the porch doorway and they entered the very well proportioned hallway, which seemed to lead to a reception room on both sides. A quick look into one then a closer look into the other indeed proved them to be identical reception or sitting rooms. Each one had a lovely open fire and a well-made fireplace and hearth. Stone, thought Joanna, nice. They had a sort of Addams style about them.

Simon smiled as he could hardly keep up with Joanna, darting from room to room. Houses were definitely her thing, unlike airstrips, which she had shown an interest in but without much depth.

The kitchen was well proportioned and had a very old, cream Aga. It looked as though, with a really good clean, it would still be in working condition. It was set in what had been a large fireplace at some time but suited the Aga fine. The units didn't look manufactured;

they looked as though someone had made them, a joiner possibly. They were very unusual, lovely warm coloured wood. Cherry, thought Joanna, although she was only guessing. Again, with a good clean they would be very serviceable. There was a large space that looked as though it had housed a dresser, which would be lovely where the space was, and was exactly what Joanna would put there. "Perfect," she said out loud, telling Simon that she hated manufactured kitchens. "Far better to have something individual that you have put your own stamp on.

"I would have a really large, pine kitchen table in the centre where you would have all your meals and you would be lovely and warm from the Aga. I wouldn't change the tiled floor because it would be perfect for the dog."

"Oh, we have a dog now?!"

"Oh, yes, of course you must have a dog, with all this space; and it would be great company for William."

Joanna went through a door that she thought would lead into the utility. However, she was amazed to find that it led into what appeared to be an annex.

"Oh, wow, I haven't even been upstairs yet and already I'm sidetracked."

"There is no hurry. You have until it turns dark to explore. Carry on, and knock yourself out."

They both explored the annex, seeing that it was a mini house, offering more or less what the ticket office did at the station, with a bedroom, lounge, kitchen and bathroom.

"Did you know that the property had an annex? Were you expecting this?"

"Well, yes, actually that's why it was on the top of my shortlist. I need somewhere close but not too close, if you get my meaning. Suitable so that Mum and Dad still have somewhere to call home and not have to say they live with their son. And vice versa – I don't want people to think I haven't left home but I want to be there for them as they are for me. Even at my age it's nice to have company."

"Oh, Simon, it's perfect, absolutely perfect. Let,s go back into the main house and have a look upstairs. From what I can see there is very little to do to make it habitable more or less straight away."

As Joanna went from room to room, three bedrooms in all and a separate bathroom and loo, she was making mental notes.

"Come on then, give me the benefit of a woman's experience and insights," challenged Simon.

"Well, I personally would put an en suite in the main bedroom; there is plenty of room if you simply knocked that cupboard out. And, do you know? Apart from decorating and carpeting it's ready to move into."

"Good grief, I don't believe it: a woman who doesn't have to spend a fortune on tearing out one interior to change it for another almost the same, but 'their own'."

"To be honest, Simon, I would give my right arm to live in a house like this," Joanna said, suddenly feeling a little embarrassed at the assumption of what she had just said.

"Would you? Would you really? Not a lot of women would want to live in such an isolated place as an airfield. The thing is it will not only suit my business purposes but I'm hoping it will also suit Dad. I hate to see him cooped up in that little room, just sitting in front of the fire. Maybe here we could get him outside into the garden, let him see some life going on with the planes coming and going. I don't know, I suppose I'm grasping at straws, but it's worth a try, isn't it?"

"Yes, yes, you're right. I feel sometimes when he sees Holly that he is about to speak. Sometimes he really looks different, as though any minute he could stand up. I think seeing the outside world could help him a lot, really I do."

As they drove back to the hotel, conversation came in short bursts about what could be done at the airfield then going silent as if both thinking about all the possibilities the property had to offer. It seemed only a matter of minutes had elapsed when they pulled back into the car park of the hotel.

Chapter 12

It was decided that they would each freshen up before meeting for the evening meal. This meant they could make their individual phone calls home to let everyone know how things were going. Although Joanna was dying to tell everyone what a wonderful time she was having and how beautiful everything was, a small part of her wanted to hold this dream, her own private interlude, to herself just for one more day.

She did call, however, and spoke to Alisha, who, as expected, wanted to know 'everything'. It took Joanna all her time to put her off, agreeing she would tell every little detail when she got home, but for now she just wanted to know if everything was okay with the girls.

"Oh, they aren't back yet, as Joel took them to see your friends Lily and William, but I will let them know you've called. And don't forget you promised first dibs on all the gen when you get back, promise?"

"Yes, yes, I promise." Joanna laughed. Part of her wanted to blurt it all out to Alisha now, but the other part wanted to keep everything that was happening close to her chest, just to give her time to savour it all.

"I have no doubt I will never be allowed to sleep until I have shared every minute detail with you all. Oh, but Alisha, I must just tell you, this is the most beautiful country and I am definitely going to bring Holly up here for a holiday when I can."

"A holiday, my, my, it must be something special girl; or is it someone special?"

Joanna laughed but didn't take the bait. As she replaced the phone, she let her mind wander, thinking it hadn't dawned on her that Simon would actually be living up here if he did decide on one of the airfields. Giving herself a quick shake, she remembered that she was supposed to be getting changed for dinner and that any minute now Simon would be knocking on her door. She had better shake a leg.

She hadn't brought anything dressy to wear but, then, she considered it really wasn't that kind of hotel. Her shower warmed her chilled body until she began to thaw out and turn pink. She hadn't been that cold since last winter, Joanna thought. Letting her memories drift back to the lovely house, in the beautiful countryside, she wondered whether it wouldn't be wonderful to live near the sea. She stopped washing herself and stood under the needles of hot water, saying out loud, "Whatever happens, I promise I will start widening my and Holly's horizons. We will go to see things and do things we have never done before, which have nothing to do with being deaf, or work. We will do it for the heck of it."

And with that said she stamped her foot in the shower tray, almost losing her balance in the process. She quickly gripped the shower rail for support.

Dressing swiftly, she decided she would put on her outfit that she had bought for the staff do. Why not? Simon wouldn't know what it had been bought for, thought Joanna. The trousers were slim-fitting dark grey, which, if she said so herself, fitted her figure to perfection.

Joanna didn't carry any excess weight and she actually had a very trim figure; she supposed the delivery of post on foot most of the route helped. The little knitted top that went with the trousers was in a shade called cherry, or so the woman in the shop had told her. She'd said it went with Joanna's colouring, although they'll say anything to make a sale. However, Joanna did think it suited her; and it looked lovely under the little charcoal woollen biker jacket she had bought to complete the outfit.

She brushed her hair thoroughly as it appeared to have a life of its own after being out on the wild and windy airfield. She didn't wear much make-up – just a little mascara. She had never found the need and, to be honest, she had always looked like a clown whenever she had allowed any of her work colleagues to show 'how fabulous you'll look'.

A quick glance in the mirror and Joanna had to look twice. There was something, something about the way she looked, not only her clothes but something else. She looked…happy. She looked a little longer and thought again to herself: Actually Joanna Berry, you look pretty good.

She gave herself a quick smile and a sarcastic twist of the lips, just as the knock on the door sounded and Simon called out, "Hey, you decent?"

Joanna opened the door, asking him what he thought she got up to on her own?

"Well, you never know with women. I have never fathomed out how it takes a woman so long to get dressed. They wear the same amount of clothes that men do, yet it takes them twice as long. Although, I must say, you appear to be the exception. You appear to be dressed," he said in a joking fashion, pretending to feign disappointment. "And may I say how nice you look? I almost said…but I didn't!…without your uniform on."

"Well, erm, thank you. I know what you mean – those uniforms are designed for men. They are certainly not designed for fashion. However, they are practical and smart, whereas your uniforms for women and men are rather more…well, lovely."

Joanna had to stop herself saying gorgeous, especially as she was picturing him in his.

"You ready? You done all your phone calls?"

"Yes, I'm ready, and yes, I did my phone call. There was only Alisha home – Joel, Precious and Holly had gone over to see your parents. Holly asked me if they could and Lily said they would be most welcome," Joanna added, just in case Simon thought it was an imposition, but instead he said he was sure his mum and dad would be very pleased to see them.

"They don't get much company since Dad's illness. It's strange how many of their friends meant to stay in touch but forgot their address, or thought maybe they had moved, or any other lame excuse rather than face the fact that Dad isn't the person they knew. But Mum is, and would love a little company. She hasn't ceased being a human being simply because poor old Dad isn't the 'helpful' solicitor he used to be.

"Oh, stop me, for goodness sake, before I rant on. When do you start doing that? I don't remember doing things like that when I was younger, did you?"

"Actually, do you know, I think I did. I think I had more courage and less awareness of making a fool of myself when I was younger. It's only as I got older and had to keep my thoughts to myself to protect the job that fed me, if you see my meaning? I'm afraid to say it, but I conformed. Kevin would have been really angry to hear me say that. We were going to be rebels, a thorn in the side of 'the establishment'. Ha ha, how the mighty have fallen."

They were sat at the table by the window in the dining room and, by the time they had finished going down memory lane, out of the window the harbour was lit up and their beams of light shone on the water. Joanna was in heaven just catching a glance out of the window.

"Did you tell Lily about the airfield and the house with the annex? Was she excited? Did you tell her I had mentally moved in, so to speak?"

"I did. Actually she told me that Joel and the girls had just left and she had lots to tell me about their visit but she was going to keep it until we get home. Now what on earth do you make of that? Anyway, I told her about the house and how you thought it was perfect; I told her about the airfield and how I thought it was perfect; and all she said was, 'Well I'm sure, between the two of you, you will do the right thing.' Ha ha, can you believe that? She is the most selfless woman. If I told her we were going to move to the moon she would just say if I thought it was right then it must be right."

"I'm pleased she enjoyed their visit. Well, I presume she enjoyed it? Ha ha, I don't suppose they could or would get up to much at your mum's, would they?"

"No, you know they wouldn't. They are wonderful girls – you and Alisha should be very proud. I know I would be. To bring up children must be hard enough but to bring up children with a disability with all the hoops you have all had to jump through just to give the girls a decent education is unbelievable. Oh God, I'm off again. I swear it's my age. Well, that's my excuse for getting irritated at life's injustices."

As they ate their meal and chatted like old friends, Joanna sensed that one or two of the other diners were more interested in them than their own partner as there appeared to be little or no conversation at their tables. Joanna didn't think Simon had even noticed. However, she herself thought how nice it was to be the couple that had so much to talk about that the time simply rushed by. On the odd 'arranged' dates she had been party to previously she had found herself half of the couple who sat straining to think of something to keep the dying conversation alive and usually failing badly.

Simon, suddenly realising that all the other diners had left and that their wine glasses were empty, asked Joanna if she would like another drink or, he offered ruefully, would she like a walk along the harbour front?

"Oh, I would love to have a walk in the fresh air; and I think one more drink and I would be tipsy. I don't drink as a rule, just the odd glass of wine at dinner."

"Fresh air? You are a glutton for punishment, but you're right. I would rather have a walk than another drink, too. I just thought you must have had as much fresh air as your lungs could handle today."

Joanna could never tell him how much she was enjoying simply being with him, being here, being part of his plans, even if it was just for now. She loved fresh air but, like his mum, she would have gone to the moon if he had asked her to at this precise moment.

As they left the hotel, Simon immediately put his arm around Joanna's shoulder and pulled her against him, allowing Joanna to breathe in his aftershave. She knew that, whatever happened in the future, she would never be able to smell Davidoff Hot Water again without thinking of him. The only reason she knew about men's cologne at all was that Alisha always bought Joel the most up-to-date smellies for Christmas.

Last Christmas she had bought Joanna Joe Malone and Joel had got his Davidoff. Joanna would never have guessed that her quick squirt of Joe Malone when she'd got dressed was having a similar effect on Simon. They walked and talked until they found themselves back at the hotel. Joanna hadn't even noticed how chilly it was until they walked into the lobby and the heat hit them.

As they reached their respective rooms, Joanna opened her door and started to unbutton her coat. Looking up at Simon, she saw a look that was unmistakably male; and, although she was out of practice, the expression in his eyes told her that he was about to kiss her. Joanna automatically lifted her face towards his. He seemed to hesitate, looking questioningly into her pale blue eyes fringed with dark lashes, as though he was about to ask permission, then his lips closed in slowly, giving Joanna the chance to turn her head if she wanted to.

As his lips touched hers, Joanna tried to savour every second, every millisecond, then she was incapable of thought any more. The kiss deepened and Joanna was beyond thought. All she could do was feel…enjoy, almost groaning with pleasure. As his lips moved firmly over Joanna's parted mouth his fingers loosened the last button on her little jacket, gaining access for his probing fingers. They began to massage her slim waistline where her top stopped and her trousers began. Suddenly aware of footsteps coming up the staircase, not knowing how he had the strength to pull away at that moment, Simon pushed Joanna gently into her room, his back facing whoever it was passing them in the corridor.

Neither of them could have said whether it was a man or a woman; they were too busy attempting to regain a vestige of control, slightly embarrassed to look into each other's eyes at how far things had moved in those few seconds. Thinking Simon would rush off to his own room after being caught in such a position, Joanna was wrong. He simply took hold of her hands and pulled her closer into him.

With his lips very close but not touching hers, he said, "I didn't take advantage of your wonderful innocence, Joanna, did I? Did I? I can't remember feeling so close to anyone for a very, very long time. I know you aren't a child, but you haven't much experience. I couldn't stop myself."

Joanna looked up from below her dark lashes that had been hiding her eyes. It was a look that told him all he needed to know, that she had more than enjoyed his kisses, and that, innocent or not, she was after all a woman.

One glance into Joanna's flushed face told Simon she had the same extraordinary feelings of closeness that he was feeling; inexplicably, as though they had known each other for a very long time.

He gave Joanna a gentle kiss on her forehead and pushed her firmly into her own room before he could take an advantage he would definitely regret at this time.

Chapter 13

Joanna lay in her comfortable warm bed soaking in all her new experiences, staring out at the navy blue sky, which was sprinkled with a million stars. The moon gave the impression of daylight it shined so brightly through her window. Joanna thought she couldn't have been happier if she'd tried. And it's not over yet, she thought. She almost hugged her body to relive the feel of Simon's arms around her, the feel of his lips on hers, her face burning red at the thought of how she had responded.

Joanna felt full, full of good things, full of wonderful experiences that she had never dreamed of two weeks ago, never thought of, to be more precise. Joanna Berry wasn't the type to be gallivanting across the country with a gorgeous man... Yes, she thought, full of...love.

No, that's impossible. Get a grip, Joanna, before you make a complete fool of yourself fawning all over the first man that shows you the slightest affection. For God's sake, woman...Joanna told herself firmly. Don't be so stupid. He probably thinks absolutely nothing about giving a woman a goodnight kiss. To him it's probably the norm. Everyone kisses nowadays. You see it all the time in all these television programmes like *Friends* or whatever – they kiss each other no matter what sex they are. But some kernel deep inside of Joanna hoped that this wasn't the case. She told herself one thing but secretly she hoped she wasn't simply a goodnight kiss out of habit; it had meant so much more to her and she would never forget it…ever.

She must have drifted off eventually, reassured by the fact that, at least if Simon did simply kiss her because it was the thing to do, he would never guess how deeply she had felt it, which meant she wouldn't have to feel embarrassed at breakfast.

Knowing she would be very cold today while they looked at another airstrip as well as going on the ferry, which Joanna guessed was likely to be an open-topped affair, she decided to dress accordingly. She showered quickly, trying not to revisit her dream of Simon's arms around her, holding her close with his lips firmly on hers, or she would never be able to leave the hot steamy shower in one piece. She dressed quickly in her black cords that suited her very well, and decided to wear the soft pink cowl-neck sweater for extra warmth. Better to be safe than sorry, she thought, remembering the previous visit to Oban airstrip. After a quick squirt of Joe Malone and pulling the brush through her hair, she admired the finished product and, feeling quite naughty, gave herself what she thought was a sexy wink.

When Simon knocked for her she opened the door wide, surprising Simon to the point where he almost fell into the open room. "I can't believe this – a woman who is not only ready but waiting? You are a rare find, Joanna Berry."

"I can't wait for another day out. This time we are even going on a ferry, something I have never ever done in my entire life. Do we leave the car at the quay?"

"No, no, we drive on to the ferry. The car comes with us, you ninny."

Joanna wasn't at all embarrassed by her mistake and didn't feel at all foolish at him calling her a ninny. After all, she told herself, there was a first time for everything, and this was hers. Next time, if ever there was one, she would be the one that knew how to do it all. And yes, she thought, there would certainly be a next time, as she fully intended to take Holly on a ferry. Oh, thought Joanna, Holly and Precious would love this.

After a calorie-busting breakfast once again, they set off for the day. They collected the car and joined the line for the ferry. Joanna could hardly contain her excitement as the cars slowly began to board the ferry, going deep into the bowels of the ship. Joanna was amazed at the sheer size of the vessel. She would never have believed that any ship could stay afloat with all the huge vehicles that were steadily filling up the decks above and below theirs. The ferry doors eventually closed with all kinds of horns and warning lights blasting at the same time, telling everyone to vacate their vehicles.

Simon guided Joanna up the narrow stairs that led to the most unexpected lounge and restaurant area. Joanna was again totally gobsmacked, as she would later tell the family back home. As they had just had breakfast and Joanna was obviously thoroughly enjoying the experience of the ferry, Simon suggested they went on to the outside deck and watched as they left Oban and would eventually reach Mull.

On the outer deck the sun was shining but it was deceptively cold and the wind was whipping at Joanna's hair. However, nothing could have induced her to stay indoors and miss the sheer pleasure of it all. Simon could see that she was enthralled by the whole experience and it gave him so much pleasure to be the one to show her what to some would be simple pleasures, but to Joanna was a life-changing experience.

Simon put his arm around Joanna's shoulder, pulling her closer for the extra warmth, he told himself, and Joanna loved the feeling of protection it gave her and the warm smell of his cologne in her nostrils. As she turned to smile directly at him, her face was the picture of happiness. She couldn't know how lovely she looked at that moment and how Simon seemed to click the camera of his mind to hold on to that look like a snapshot for his memory only. They began to draw closer to the island, with Simon pointing out elements of interest, then all too soon the claxon sounded and they were being told to board their vehicles ready for departure.

As they pulled off the ferry and on to the island, Joanna was enthralled by the beauty and remoteness of her surroundings, while Simon followed his instructions as to where exactly the airstrip was. It didn't really take much finding as the island wasn't very large. However, it was becoming increasingly obvious to Simon that the journey to get to and from the mainland would be fine for him but would be more challenging if, for medical reasons, his mother and father needed to cross. He had researched the medical care on Mull, though, and the new Mull and Iona Health Services were by all accounts excellent.

They came across the entrance to the airstrip but there was no sign of a control tower. In fact, the entrance looked as though the gate hadn't been opened for a very long time. However, thought Simon, that's what makes it so affordable; he would try not to make any judgements until he had seen the whole package.

As they drove up a very rickety single track that had more grass than tarmac, Simon's eyes darted from side to side taking in the relative lack of outbuildings – those that were there were barely standing. Joanna heard Simon sigh but said nothing. They drove a little farther to where they could see a little wooden office type building at the end of what looked as though it had once been a runway, but even Joanna had a sinking feeling about this one. They parked the car and started towards what appeared to be a hangar, but as they got closer it became pretty obvious that it was simply a shell. What had looked to be a fairly substantial building on the Internet was in reality just a wreck.

Simon took a deep sigh again, saying that he was beginning to think this one was a wash-out. He had no doubt that, in its day, it had been a decent little airstrip for the size of the island. "But," he continued, "the fact that there is more land with this one doesn't help with knowing that you would have to spend a fortune on it to bring it up to any kind of usable condition."

Joanna ventured a small utterance so as not to annoy Simon when he was clearly disappointed, asking if there was a house with this one.

"No. To be honest, this was my wild card. There is more land with this strip and it's less than half the price of the one in Oban. I thought I could make a killing in the island-hopping style of courier work. That would mean I wasn't away from home for any long periods of time. My intention was to buy a kit-form property and have a team of builders erect it before I moved Mum and Dad up here. However," he said a little disappointedly, "it doesn't have the appeal of the strip at Oban. I know it's less money, with my business head on, but, to be honest, it is too far gone, and I think if you weren't careful it could become a money pit. Judging by the stuff in the office-come-workshop, some sort of company worked out of that strip but not for a lot of years, which is why the only runway looks more like a lawn bowling green than an airstrip. It's a shame, because I think I could probably get a lot of work from the likes of Tobermory, Bunessan and many of the smaller islands."

"Could you not still get that business even if you flew out of Oban?" asked Joanna. "Surely for small companies, such as those who specially export trout, et cetera from Tobermory…? If I'm not mistaken I've delivered in my post van to customers in Derby, would you believe? It's only a suggestion, and I realise, from what little we have seen of Mull, that it is slightly more remote than Oban; but, possibly, if you were on your own, building the business and able to rough it at first, this may be the better buy financially." Joanna added that, in her humble opinion, it did look as though it could become a bit of a money pit to her as well.

As they were mulling over the condition of the buildings, Simon's mobile rang. He had almost forgotten he had a phone with him, but he answered.

"Hello, yes? Mum, is that you? I'm only getting every other word, Mum, is there something wrong?"

A voice that seemed a long way off and crackled over each sentence said, "No, eh, no, everything's fine. I just wondered when you would be back."

At least that was what Simon thought she'd said, although he couldn't get every word. He asked again, "Are you sure there isn't anything wrong? Is Dad all right?"

Lily said, "Yes, he's fine. Don't worry, you'll see him when you get back. It's nothing I can't handle—" The phone went dead.

"Did she sound worried? Do you think there is something wrong, or was she simply ringing for a chat?"

"No, she was being 'brave' again, and I'm sure there is something up as Mum doesn't ring for nothing. She hates to bother me about anything, that's the problem. I have to read between the lines. Hence the reason I arrived home unexpectedly, remember, when you leapt out at me from the wood shed," Simon teased in an attempt at humour in order to look as though he wasn't unduly worried about his parents. However, after a few moments of thought, he announced that they had better make their way back to the ferry terminal.

"I feel it in my water, something is up. Listen, what do you say we get back to the hotel and pack…?"

"Yes, you're right. If there is anything wrong you would never forgive yourself if you weren't there. We can share the driving if one of us becomes too tired."

"Don't worry about that; I'm used to doing very long-haul flights. I manage without sleep for twenty-four to thirty-six hours on a regular basis, but thank you for the offer."

Joanna was trying so hard not to be disappointed as her adventure was fast coming to a close. But she scolded herself – how thoughtless is that, Joanna Berry? You've had a wonderful few days, and seen some amazing sights; how can you be so selfish? A little part of Joanna wanted to be selfish, but Joanna the caring person knew she would never settle and neither would Simon. Yet, oh, she would never forget these few days, ever…

Going back to the mainland from Mull was interesting but it was as though a blanket had fallen on their newly formed friendship, as Simon was understandably quiet. Arriving back at the hotel Simon didn't take the car to the car park but simply parked out front as they weren't going to take long to throw their clothes into their bags and be off.

Chapter 14

The journey back seemed much swifter than the journey up, and as darkness fell there was no scenery for Joanna to see. She had been staring out of the window thinking about her short break from reality and how very soon she would return to her old life. Was that going to be enough? she mused. Would she be able to slot right back into the groove as though there was nothing out there but the Peak District? Beautiful though it was, it had its limits.

Simon was also mulling things over in his mind, firstly what he was going to face this time when he arrived home. It couldn't be the roof or anything like that; Mum wouldn't ring for that. It had to be Dad. Then he thought about the two airstrips he had seen and, yes, Joanna was right. Had he been a bit younger and didn't have to worry about somewhere to live until the business was up and running, he could have lived in a caravan on the Mull site. He wouldn't mind so much now, but his parents couldn't turn the clock back. They needed comfort now; they needed support from him, which was why this property choice was all important.

"It has to be the Oban strip," Simon suddenly said out loud, making Joanna jump.

"Oh, sorry, I'm weighing things up in my mind, the pros and the cons. My priority has to be living accommodation for Mum and Dad, and I don't mean that in a martyred way. After all, isn't that the very reason why I'm moving back home?"

"Well, it must be your decision, Simon, but if you don't mind an opinion I would gladly chip in my four-penn'orth."

"No, no, fire away. I think I've made my decision, but it's always worth a second opinion; and, after all, you have been good enough to give up your holiday to help me out, so go ahead."

"Well, first of all, I certainly haven't given anything up; on the contrary you have given me the holiday of a lifetime… I know I know you think a holiday of a lifetime is a cruise or something. Well I have to tell you that this to me beats any of your long-haul holidays abroad, and… I will always remember these few days. Anyway, back to the business in hand, and just say if you think it's rubbish."

"I will. Now tell me what you think, for goodness sake."

Joanna told him, "Well, if you want to spend time with your parents – which is the whole reason you're looking for these opportunities in England or Scotland rather than abroad, isn't it? – then the site on Mull would, in my amateur estimation, take at least five years to become operational with the correct outbuildings, repairs to the runway, office and warehouse facilities, not to mention a hangar large enough to house your planes each winter. I'm only guessing, but, by the simple fact that Mull is an island, it seems possible that there may not be the snow, but what about the winds and the rain? Again, from my limited experience, you would have problems flying in windy conditions, so you may lose a fair few days to bad weather conditions. Then the biggie of the lot is the accommodation for your parents. With the best will in the world, Simon, even with a brilliant team of builders, you're still talking the better part of a year to erect any house.

"On the other hand, the set-up at Oban is ready-made and could be up and running within weeks. You could move your parents almost straight into the house. It needs a bit of decorating, but that wouldn't take a professional decorator long. The whole strip looked in working order to my untrained eye and the hangars, you said so yourself, were in perfect nick."

Joanna lifted her hands, palms up, saying, "*Voilà*! Or Bob's your uncle," she laughed, and waited for Simon to disagree and make loads of 'ah, buts'.

Instead, he said, "I couldn't agree more. That's another thing that makes you unusual – a woman who actually looks at a problem logically without throwing money at it in the hope that it will make it better. Actually, that was my decision, too, so we are in total agreement."

Simon seemed a lot happier as he drove. Now all he had to worry about was his mother's problem. He had given her another ring when they'd returned to the hotel but she had been most insistent that it was nothing she couldn't handle and that he was to enjoy his time away. This made Simon worry all the more.

He wasn't overly concerned about her handling the situation – despite the way it may have looked, he did have full confidence in his mother's ability. If it hadn't been for his mother their solicitor's practice would have gone down the tubes after his father took ill. He knew that she had wound the business up, and found a buyer for it at the right price, not a panic sale. She looked after his father, bless her, but she had an independent streak that stopped her from calling on Simon when she needed help. She always thought she was bothering him.

Simon decided that stopping for something to eat and a coffee wasn't going to make them much later and it was silly to drive on without a rest so they stopped at a Little Chef not far outside Carlisle. As they ate their meal, not in silence but deep in thought, Joanna told herself that she would not be depressed that her little trip was over, In fact, she decided that it would spur her on to do other trips…although she had to admit even to herself that it wouldn't be the same.

It had begun to dawn on Joanna that she seemed to be inordinately attracted to this tall, dark, handsome man. She hoped it was simply a crush and that she would quickly get over it, as nothing could possibly come of it.

"Hey, you've gone all quiet again. I'm sorry to have dashed you home in such a hurry. But we would have been coming home tomorrow anyway, and you're right, I wouldn't forgive myself if there was anything wrong at home."

He took hold of Joanna's hand in his, saying, "I want you to know how grateful I am to you, Joanna Berry. You are a rare find in this day and age, and I have enjoyed your company, enjoyed showing you things you had never seen before."

He gave her hand a slight squeeze before moving to stand up, and on that note they left to restart their journey.

Chapter 15

In the darkness, the hum of the engine and the warmth from the heater conspired to lull Joanna into a dreamlike place. She could hear the radio in the background but she seemed miles away, comfortable and content. Then a gentle shaking movement and Simon's voice was telling her they were almost home made Joanna's eyes shoot open.

"Home, already? God, I'm so sorry. I was going to share the driving, you should have woken me. A fine co-pilot I would make."

As Simon swung the car into the drive of the old yard, the front door seemed to pop open within seconds. Simon was amazed, but Joanna told him that his mum had a chair strategically placed at the window so that she saw everything, and she must have seen the lights through the curtains.

As they climbed out of the car, Lily came out to meet them. Her excitement was evident, so, whatever had happened, it wasn't bad, thought Simon, thanking his lucky stars for that. They reached the front door and went inside.

Then Lily couldn't contain it any longer. "Oh, Simon, Joanna, you aren't going to believe me when I tell... Oh, you didn't travel back at this hour because of me, did you? Oh, I hope you didn't... But, oh, I must tell you this."

"Calm yourself, Mum, for goodness sake, you'll have a heart attack. Just tell us slowly."

"I will. Oh, Joanna, your friend, the doctor friend? He came and he brought the girls, you know?"

Joanna nodded that she knew, telling Lily to carry on.

"Well, Holly and Precious... Oh, Precious, isn't she sweet? Well, anyway, they went straight to William and took hold of his hands and, as I was talking to the doctor...erm, I mean Joel, they asked if they could take William for a walk... Ah, wasn't that nice of them? Just as I was going to say that William didn't walk, blow me if he didn't stand up holding their hands and walk towards the door! I couldn't believe my eyes; I still can't believe it. But, but that's not all. They took him out into the drive and they walked all the way round the yard and then brought him back. Oh, and Simon, Joanna, you know what they said? They said they didn't want to tire him out so he should sit down and have a rest now.

"But you know, as your doctor friend and I watched the girls walking William slowly round the yard… I saw something. I saw a flicker of a change in his face. It's hard to explain, but for the last three years his face has been a total blank. Yet, while he was with the girls, it was as though a switch had been thrown and he had life in his face. Oh, I'm not saying he had full expression, but I know it was there," she said positively. "And that wonderful man, the doctor, Joel (he said to call him that), he doesn't think that William had a conventional stroke. He said it isn't his field, though. He is ENT, you know," she informed Joanna as if she didn't know.

"But he said he would make some enquiries with a friend of his and arrange some tests for William. He said he thought that William had some sort of 'locked in syndrome' that is a type of illness that could have been brought on by stress or overwork. Oh, I'm so grateful to you and your friends, Joanna. William has sat in that chair for almost three years without so much as a flicker of interest until the day Holly held his hand. Now I know he will get better, I just know it. Maybe not the same as he was, but I'm sure now."

Lily hugged Joanna, saying she just knew everything was going to change…and for the better. Joanna and Simon were both totally gobsmacked. Joanna was so happy that Joel had taken the girls or William might never have been seen by a doctor who cared enough. Simon was blown away to think what a difference it would make to see his father, see the face and the expressions he remembered. He had always felt, since his dad's illness, that it was his personality and his soul that had been lost.

It was obvious to all of them that they ought not to get too carried away by this change, but, that said, it was impossible not to get excited. William had shown absolutely no sign of any change in three years, so this had to be a breakthrough.

As they were all still reeling with the excitement of Lily's news, a voice coming from the door broke into their euphoria, saying, "Darling, you should have waited for me, I would have travelled with you. Oh, don't mind me, I saw the car lights from your little house and couldn't wait for you to come round."

As all three pairs of eyes shot towards the sound, Joanna's eyes must have opened the widest, as there in the doorway was what could only be described as a half-naked woman. Well, she did have on what would have passed for a negligee if anyone still wore them anymore, but it was very thin – flimsy, one would say. In fact, it was almost see-through, but you didn't have to see through it: you simply had to look at the curves and the bosom that was attempting to escape to know she was buck-naked underneath.

Joanna's mouth had literally fallen open and she vaguely heard Lily comment in the background, quietly saying that this was the slight problem she didn't want to tell you about. This was directed at Simon.

The diaphanous cloud of silk made a beeline for Simon, putting her arms around his neck and kissing him full on the lips, saying she had missed him, but that his kind mother had let her into Simon's part of the house and she had made herself comfortable.

Simon had recovered his equilibrium by this time and quickly attempted to introduce the woman who was draped around his neck. He seemed to peel her off slightly, allowing a little space between so that he could carry out the introductions.

"Erm, Lydia, how…nice to see…you. How unexpected."

"Well, darling, I don't know why you should be surprised. You know, as your 'partner' naturally I want to be with you at all stages of the new business and I thought you might have needed this."

Lydia held up a small green card out of what seemed to be thin air, as she certainly didn't have any pockets.

"My licence! Where on earth? How have you got my licence? You have no idea how much trouble it has caused."

"Darling, it must have fallen out of your wallet. I found it on our bedroom floor, so I thought I'd better come straight up as I knew you would need it to hire a car. Your mother said your postlady hired a car for you temporarily – how nice. Oh, you must be her, how kind."

Lily seemed to remember her attitude from her former life when she had dealt with many unsavoury clients, as she sniped quite curtly towards the voluptuous figure hanging on to Simon's arm, "Joanna is not simply our postlady; she is also a very, very dear friend, isn't she, Simon?"

Simon was still slightly in shock. However, he had recovered enough to repeat what his mother had said, saying that Joanna had been wonderful and had given up her holiday to accompany him while he looked at the sites. "I couldn't have managed without Joanna, and she has been a great help to our legal problems, being a newly qualified lawyer."

"Oh, hardly, I have a law degree, but I'm not yet practising."

"How nice. Then you can stop being a postie and do a proper job, that'll be nice for you. Well, I can't thank you enough…er, Joan, did you say?"

"Joanna," said Joanna, sensing the chill of dislike dripping off the naked lady's tongue. Time, she thought, to make a quick exit before it hit her that Simon shared a bedroom with that…person.

"Well, it's been nice meeting you, Miss…?"

"Lydia. Lydia Cooper. Yes, same here. In case we don't meet again, bye."

As Joanna made towards the door she could feel her face starting to flush and, for some inexplicable reason, a lump was beginning to form in her throat. She knew she simply had to get to the car where she would be safe. Lily began to move towards the door, and Simon made to come see her off, but Joanna said quickly over her shoulder, "No, no, stay with your guest. I'm fine. I'll no doubt see you later on in the week on my rounds," and with that she hurried towards the front door and out to the car.

Lily, however, hurried the best she could with her plaster on her foot, saying into the open window as Joanna was adjusting the seat and turning on the lights for a quick exit, "Thank you, Joanna, thank you so much for all you've done. We will see you for coffee as usual, won't we? William and I so look forward to it. And Joanna… Simon has never told me about 'her' so I don't believe they are an 'item'."

This was said with a query as if she wasn't sure if it was the right terminology. Joanna gave a weak smile, assuring Lily she would definitely be seeing both herself and Holly once she was back to work. She waved automatically to Lily and pulled off the drive and into the night.

Chapter 16

A woman? There was a woman in Simon's life? That was something Joanna had never contemplated. He had said he was lonely on his long-haul flights and how in his job he never had the chance to meet anyone with whom to have a relationship. I suppose she works with him and that must be how they met? Is she a pilot? wondered Joanna, or an air stewardess? She said she was his partner… Did she mean partner as in couple or business partner? All these questions were rattling around in Joanna's head as she drove home in the darkness.

All of a sudden, her wonderful experience had become soured. She chided herself for being silly. It wasn't as though she meant anything to Simon. I mean, she thought, he couldn't know that I have a gigantic crush on him. She was surprising herself by even thinking about it, but it was true. She supposed she hadn't felt like that since… Oh God, it was so long ago she couldn't remember, but she had began to feel like she had when she was with Kevin, except this time without the gung-ho attitude of a student. A slightly more adult and grown-up feeling, she mused.

She couldn't deny there was attraction on her side, but was she only kidding herself that she had seen attraction in his eyes towards her? Holiday romance, don't they call it? Well, that'll teach you, Joanna Berry, to stop throwing your heart at the first good-looking guy that comes along. Had she learned nothing since Kevin? Although no one could have said Kevin was handsome, he did have a boyish charm that had made him interesting and lovable. Simon had magnetism, coupled with devastatingly good looks. Who was she kidding? He was gorgeous and she was just upset because he appeared to be taken and he had never mentioned it to her.

Still wrestling with her disappointment and irrational thoughts about that awful woman sharing Simon's life, his house, his courier business, Lily and William's lives, she almost missed the drive. Thinking she was in the little van, she narrowly missed the lawn. As she jammed the brakes on and turned the engine off, yanking the handbrake on, Joanna said out loud, "Damn it, Simon, she's horrible. She looks more like the evil side of Dolly Parton (not that Dolly has an evil side but you know what I mean). She's…erm…sexy and…erm…sarcastic and…and… I don't like her. How dare she call me a 'postie', like I was some sort of char lady?"

As she entered the house, thinking everyone was in bed as at first she saw no lights on, she dropped her bag on the floor, promising to deal with it in the morning. She knew she wouldn't be ready for sleep after napping in the car on the way home; plus her brain was lit up like a Christmas tree just thinking about 'her'.

Joanna decided to have a mug of hot chocolate to knock herself out. It usually did the trick. However, as she walked into the kitchen, she saw the light on in the lounge and popped her head round the door very quietly. She saw Joel and Alisha lying spooned together on the sofa fast asleep. She crept out into the kitchen to put the kettle on. Then, while she sat at the kitchen table, seemingly in a world of her own, a sleepy voice behind her said, "Hey, you're home? We didn't expect you until tomorrow sometime, is everything okay?"

"Oh hi. Yes, yes, everything's fine," Joanna said with a painted smile spread all over her face that Alisha immediately recognised. She sat next to Joanna at the table and waited while giving that look that says 'Tell…'.

"No really, I've had a wonderful time. You would love Scotland, Lish, you really would. The scenery, the sea views; and, oh, I can't begin to tell you what a wonderful time I've had."

"Mmm, huh, well, if that's the case, why do you look like you lost a pound and found a penny? What happened to change your wonderful experience? Mmm?"

Joanna started by saying, "Oh, it's late and I'm sure you're tired, and Joel is still asleep on the sofa, isn't he?"

Alisha said there was no way; she had sent him up to bed while she got the lowdown on Joanna's trip away with the gorgeous Simon.

"And he went without knowing all the details?"

"Well, he did, but he knows that I will tell him all the highlights in the morning. Now come on, spill the beans, lady."

Joanna told Alisha about the wonderful hotel, the scenery, about both the airstrips and how she had given her opinion, which apparently was the same as his, et cetera, and then her voice slowed slightly. She said everything was great until they had got a phone call from Lily. Simon had been very worried because Lily was telling him everything was fine but he was sure it wasn't, so they had decided to travel back after they caught the ferry back to Oban to collect their clothes from the hotel.

"You had separate rooms, then?"

"Lisha! Of course we had separate rooms, what on earth do you think we are?"

"Young, human, good-looking, normal, hot-blooded people, that's what."

"Well, we did have separate rooms. Mine overlooked the harbour and the view was fantastic."

"And?"

"Oh God, you won't be happy, will you, until I tell you everything? Will you?"

"I knew it! I knew it. Now spill it, sister," said Alisha, rubbing her hands together in anticipation.

Joanna took a deep breath, thinking back to the first kiss, almost closing her eyes to feel it all over again.

"Come on, come on, I'm going to burst if you don't tell me."

So Joanna began to tell her how it had been so fleeting she hardly knew it had happened, but that the kiss at the top of the stairs when they were interrupted had been so much more sustaining, and it gave her something to rewind and relive all over again.

"So how far do you think it would have gone if you hadn't been interrupted, eh? Eh?"

Joanna blushed, having told too much, she thought to herself. It hadn't really sunk in yet, and, really, had she not been pushed she would have kept it her own private secret for a while longer, like a treasure you hid away and looked at once in a while in private. "Anyway," she ploughed on, "we came back tonight rather than tomorrow.

"Oh, and Lily met us on the drive and told us all about Joel and the girls' visit. Oh, Lish, she is so thrilled; you can tell she is lit up with hope for William. Who would have thought it: the two girls taking off for a walk like that, eh, and him following? Does Joel really think he can get someone to help him?"

"Oh, yes, he has spoken to someone at the hospital. William will be getting an appointment soon. He definitely thinks, with the improvements and the progress he has made in only a couple of weeks, that there is a good chance that he may make a partial recovery in some form or other."

"Oh, Lisha, I couldn't be more happy for Lily and William and…um, Simon, of course."

This last bit was said with a tinge of sadness in her voice, which Lisha heard. She put her hand on Joanna's arm, saying gently, "And what else happened to make you so down instead of climbing the walls with excitement?"

Joanna began to tell her of the moment of pure euphoria when they were told of William's prognosis. "Then I looked up to see Cruella Deville, lounging against the door almost stark naked. Then she threw herself at Simon… God, Lish, you should have seen her. I was gobsmacked and, to be honest, so was Simon. She even had his licence; she said it must have fallen out of his wallet on to 'their' bedroom floor!

"Poor Lily hadn't wanted to tell us about 'her'. Apparently she just arrived and Lily had to put her up so she put her in Simon's part of the house. She must have seen the car lights and hot-footed it over… She called me a postie! Can you believe it, the cheeky bitch? She more or less dismissed me! And another thing – she is apparently his partner!"

"His partner? Do you mean as in live-in partner, or business partner?"

"I don't know, she just said partner. But if they share a bed then I suppose you can assume it's both."

"Strange – that's not the impression I got of Simon. I got the impression he was a bit lonely, and he never mentioned a partner. Listen, Joanna, this woman might have got her feathers ruffled when she heard from Lily that Simon had gone away with another woman, and you don't really know the full story, now, do you? You haven't spoken to Simon on your own, so try not to judge him, will you? Remember how nice he was with the girls; and I don't think he would have kissed you like that if he already had a little woman at home."

Joanna said it was ridiculous anyway, for goodness sake, she was only someone who had helped him out. What was she thinking? She had no claim on him. What's a kiss in a doorway for God's sake? She was immature and should grow up and not read too much into it, and just think of it as a wonderful holiday with a wonderful guide.

Saying and believing were two different things, as Joanna knew, but she would simply have to get over it. One thing she did know, though, was that her life would never be the same, though, actually, she didn't want to go back to simply being Joanna the postlady anymore.

Alisha stood up, patting Joanna's hand as she sat in her thoughtful mood, but, as she got to the door, she suddenly stopped and said, "Hey, you never told me what exactly did Cruella look like? I mean minus the horns and the tail?"

"Well, if I try to blot out her enormous bosom, which I may say is very hard to do, I would have to say… Grudgingly… And it pains me to say it…"

"Yes, yes, get on with it. She was obviously a beauty?"

"Well, if you like that sort of thing. She has long black hair, and, actually I cannot tell a lie, she is good-looking… But she has a vamp sort of way with her, you know?"

"A vamp? Joanna Berry, what on earth do you know about vamps?"

"Well, you know, sort of forward and tarty, if you know what I mean?"

Knowing that Joanna was hurting inside, even though she wasn't going to admit it, Alisha said, "Yes, I know the type, and do you know something for nothing, Joanna? I don't believe for one minute that she is Simon's type. No, sir, the Simon we've met is not the type who would fall for a pushy woman, take my word for it."

And, with that, she left. Joanna decided she didn't want hot chocolate now, after all. She didn't want to force sleep; she wanted to mull over what Alisha had said and compare it with her impressions of Simon and Cruella.

Chapter 17

Joanna must have eventually dropped off to sleep. She was woken by a light tap on her shoulder, and, for a split second before she opened her eyes, a tiny part of her mind imagined it was Simon. She drowsily turned over to face the voice that said, "Mum, will you be up before I go to school or are you sleeping late?" in the way that kids do when they wake you up. With no chance of ever getting back into that slumberous place you left, you are rudely dragged from it.

Joanna said, "Hi," through a haze of sleep, with her head almost buried under the duvet and just enough showing so that Holly could read her lips. Joanna was all snuggled under the duvet with it wrapped around her neck and really didn't feel like facing the world yet, never mind the million questions and innuendo from two girls of a certain age who had suddenly developed an interest in her private life. Oh, thought Joanna, a private life, what's one of those?

She knew that she would never sleep now and that she may as well get up and get it over with. But that wasn't really nice – the girls were only interested... Well, in Simon they were interested. And Joanna did want to tell Holly all about her holiday, so she threw the duvet back and asked Holly just to give her five minutes to brush her teeth.

Sat at the kitchen table with the smell of fresh coffee, she pulled herself together, as she usually did very quickly. She was actually a morning person, unlike many. The girls were sitting 'agog' for all the info.

"Well..." Joanna said, stretching out the anticipation to excite the girls. "It was wonderful. Oh, the scenery, the sea, the hotel – you would have loved it, and, oh, you wouldn't believe what I saw on the way? We stopped at a place called Carter Bar, which is the sort of gateway to Scotland on one side of the road, and on the other side of the road it's the gateway back into England. And standing there on a stone plinth was a man playing bagpipes. Honestly, he had on a kilt and everything. Oh, you should have seen it.

"We went to both airstrips and they were really interesting, but the thing that was most fascinating for me was watching the boats coming in and out of the harbour and the ferry ride over to the island of Mull itself."

"And did anyone live on the island," one of the girls asked, "or was it deserted? Were you the only ones there?"

"No, no, it wasn't deserted. It had houses and buses and little shops and villages. It was quite a large island, I suppose, as islands go. But a little bit too remote for William and Lily.

"Oh, you have just reminded me about both of you girls taking William for a walk... How wonderful, I can't believe it! He just simply stood up, Lily says, and you walked out of the door and into the yard. I am so proud of both of you; and now William is going to see a specialist?"

"I spoke to a friend of mine at the hospital and he is going to send for William very soon," said Joel, who was standing over the stove, cooking breakfast for everyone. It was such a treat on a school day as Joel would normally be at work and so would Joanna, but today was like a holiday for them all.

"You are a treasure, Joel, for doing that for Lily and William. I'm so glad you could take the girls or you would never have met him and he would have sat there forever. Poor William, so you think it's possible it wasn't a conventional stroke then and there is a possibility he may regain some sort of normality?"

"Well, as I told Lily, it's not my field, but, in my opinion, he has made such improvements in a very short space of time… Well, since he met Holly basically. I think something in Holly triggered a response and… Well, I don't know, but the human mind is a complex thing. If he had a nervous breakdown or mini stroke, well, it may simply be that he has been locked inside and Holly was the one able to flip the switch… I'm only making a guess, but, hopefully, it's an informed guess and I'm right."

Holly and Precious both signed and spoke excitedly at the same time, saying how wonderful William was and how they had taken him for a walk. Then they looked at each other and laughed. Knowing they would have to go to school soon and they needed to know all the 'gen', both girls chimed in together, asking, "But what was it like with Simon…?"

"Now, what could you possibly mean by that?" Joanna said, feigning ignorance.

"Was he lovely and was he gentlemanly, like a film star?"

"Mmm, well, yes, he was gentlemanly, and…erm… We had good fun and he looked after me and he was very nice."

The girls weren't satisfied with that explanation and wanted more, persisting, "But you do like him, though, don't you? And he is like a film star, isn't he?"

Joanna didn't realise she had actually given herself away by slightly hesitating. With a lift of the eyebrow, she imagined, if he were a film star, who he would be. George Clooney, she thought. Oh my God. She coughed and said, "Film star? Oh, you mean like a pop singer or something?"

"No, a man from a film. You know, like…erm…Johnny Depp. Do you not think he's handsome like Johnny Depp?"

The girls stared with wide eyes at Joanna, waiting for her reaction, which they thought would show she had instantly fallen in love with a Johnny Depp look-alike while on holiday in Scotland. Joanna laughed, trying not to form an image of George Clooney or Johnny Depp in her mind, or they would be convinced she was passionately in love with Simon's look-alike.

She knew she was going to have to say something just to get them off her back. She knew they would never give up, so she gave them a little to keep them happy.

"Well… He is lovely in his own way, and yes, I can see what you mean about being a film star look-alike. And yes, he did treat me very well – better, I think, than most film stars of today would have. Now, is that enough? Will you let me get dressed now and will you go to school? Please?"

The last of the breakfast was swallowed hurriedly, Joel saying in his good-natured banter, "Well, is that it? I cook you wonderful breakfast and now I'm off to do the school run and I don't get so much as a kiss or thank you from anyone. I'm just a slave around here. Do you know that slavery is alive and well and living in this house?"

Just as he was about to theatrically flounce out of the kitchen, throwing his flowered apron on a nearby chair, he turned back, saying to Joanna, "Keep the kettle hot, I'll be back in no time at all." With an outrageous wink, he added, "And you can tell me the grown-up version."

Rolling their eyes and making suggestive faces, the girls giggled their way to the front door and out to the car.

Chapter 18

Joanna decided that, as today was her last day before going back to work, she would sort her washing and do some housework. She thought that she should also make the evening meal. After all, she had been the one who had been away for a wonderful holiday, leaving poor Joel and Alisha to do everything. Not that they minded in the least.

Also, if she filled her day with lots of jobs to do, it would give her less time to brood over Cruella Deville. She was determined not to let her spoil the memory of her time with Simon and those fleeting kisses… Within seconds of thinking of Simon's lips pressed against hers, she was transported back outside her bedroom door with Simon's hands burning a trail on her skin. The weakness in her legs and a feeling in the pit of her stomach, gave her what could only be described as a bit of a zing, not a feeling she remembered. It was so long ago that she hardly recognised it as sexual attraction.

It wasn't until she heard Joel coming in the front door, talking away to himself as usual about the hire car, that she suddenly said, "Oh, sh… I forgot all about that."

"So when will you be taking the hire car back to the rental place then?"

Joanna sighed; she had forgotten all about the car. That meant she would have to see 'her' again. "Oh no," she repeated. "Well, I want to do one or two jobs this morning."

"Maybe they will still need you today for something."

"No, they won't. 'She' has a car."

"Oh, well, that's okay then. I just thought they may think, seeing as you already had the hire car, you would take them," said Joel innocently, but very quickly changed his tone when Joanna gave him the look that said, 'Never in a million years'; the type of look Alisha gave him when she came in from a night shift to find Joel in an amorous mood. He soon got the message, saying, "Well, maybe you should ring him, then, save you going round?" It was obvious to Joel that Joanna didn't want to go to the house in case she ran into Simon's lady friend. But he didn't say that out loud… Oh no, thought Joel. That's one thing I've learned about women, never to get involved, because you are always in the wrong.

"Yes, yes, you're right, that's what I'll do. It's silly to go traipsing around and disturbing them if he doesn't need me today, isn't it?" Joanna said out loud in an attempt to convince both herself and Joel. However, she was fooling no one. It was obvious to anyone that Joanna simply couldn't face seeing Simon and Lydia together. Having built herself up, having all the words formed that she would use when she spoke to him… The number was engaged. She mentally let out a sigh of relief, but after three times she was beginning to get irritated. She tried one more time, but, by this time, she had given up all hope of ever getting through. Suddenly the phone was answered, and Lily's voice said hello and gave her number.

"Oh, er, hello, Lily. Sorry, you caught me off guard. I've been trying to get through for some time, but you appear to have been engaged.

"Yes," Lily responded, "Simon got a call from Gatwick, his base, this morning, and ever since he has been on and off the phone. It must have been important because he took the calls in my bedroom and closed the door. So what that's all about, I don't know. Anyway, I'm drivelling again. What can I do for you, my dear?"

"Well, actually, it's Simon I need to speak to, unless you can take a message to him. It's just I wanted to know if I should take the hire car back to the depot today or will he need it for himself and...Lydia?" Joanna almost choked on her name.

Lily suggested she would go and ask Simon then she would ring back. The phone rang a few minutes later, but, to Joanna's surprise, it was Simon's rich voice.

"Hi, Joanna, Simon here. Listen, I've spoken to the hire firm and paid the bill with my credit card, so if you wouldn't mind returning the car some time before lunch that would be much appreciated. We have Lydia's car at the moment and I can always hire another car if need be."

Simon's voice was firm but it had none of its usual warmth; in fact, if anything he seemed distracted. Joanna simply agreed, saying it was no problem. She thanked him for her holiday in Scotland and hoped his business venture went well. She rang off, saying, "Bye, Simon," knowing that was almost certainly the last she would see of him.

As she sat still, holding the phone in her hand, suddenly, out of nowhere, tears sprang up into her blue eyes, blurring her vision. That's right, she thought: in a few short weeks, when he sorts his business out then takes William and Lily up to Scotland, I won't ever see him again.

"Hey, you want coffee, or are you dashing out, Joanna?"

Joanna swallowed hard, calling back in as normal a voice as possible that she wouldn't bother. She said, as she began up the stairs, "I'd better get a move on if I have to get this car back before lunchtime."

Joanna went into the bathroom and rinsed her face. Looking into the mirror at the face that only a few short weeks ago was delightfully oblivious to the outside world, she thought to herself, why, oh why had she had a glimpse of what was out there if for her it was unattainable? It seemed cruel that she had been happy in her ignorance, but now that she had taken a bite of the cherry and wanted more, it was being snatched away… Again.

Big fat tears threatened to spill over again until Joanna scrubbed her face with cold water to obliterate any traces. She gave herself a mental shake and decided she would leave her little jobs for later; she would take the car back to the rental place first. It would give her a chance to compose herself before anyone saw how silly she was being.

Because that's all it is, thought Joanna: you are feeling sorry for yourself. He never promised anything, she remonstrated with herself. To him, he was simply being a gentleman and thought it was expected of him to give her a quick peck before sending her off to bed. She didn't know why she was making such a big deal out of it. "God, am I that frustrated?" Was that what she had become? A frustrated single mother? Before long, she continued to herself, she would be 'a woman of a certain age'.

This gets worse, she thought. I must pull myself together. If I'm not happy with life as it is then I will simply have to change it. I'll start dating again, she told herself, knowing that, all the time and for ever more, she would compare every man she ever went out with against Simon.

She arrived at the rental place and decided once she had dropped the car off she may as well collect her van for the morning. She tried not to think about the last time she had been at the rental company, when she was with Simon, and they had been fresh from their triumph with the roofing company. She remembered how they had laughed then attempted to fool the woman on the rental desk that they were a couple in order to hire in Joanna's name.

As she parked the car and went into the office to return the keys she needn't have worried about any explanations as this time a very efficient young man took the keys and confirmed that the car had been paid for in full.

Joanna decided she would walk the short distance to the Post Office depot and collect her van. Calling into the office to collect her keys, she found a note attached that explained that her run had been changed for the following week to cover for holiday entitlement. Joanna read the note twice to make sure she wasn't mistaken. Part of her was disappointed that the decision seemed to be out of her hands. She was actually destined not to see Simon, William or Lily. But one thing she did know was that, whatever happened, she had to stop brooding about it and pull herself together.

Chapter 19

All too soon Joanna was back to collecting her mail from the depot for her new route. Once she started her round Joanna soon got back into the swing of it. She had actually done this run before and if she wasn't mistaken it took her very close to Kevin's parents' house. She decided that if she put a spurt on she would have time to call in and have a coffee and a chat with them. Well, chat was a bit of an exaggeration; it was more like charades, but they always managed to make themselves understood.

As Joanna pulled the little van into the street where Harry and Harriet lived, she was instantly taken back by the For Sale sign in the rather overgrown garden. Joanna was shocked, firstly, by what had happened to the garden – it had been Harry's pride and joy – and secondly, why was the house up for sale? As she parked the van and walked up the path it became increasingly obvious that the house wasn't lived in. Oh, there were curtains at the windows but it was obvious that there was nobody at home. Peering through the window, she felt her fears were confirmed: there was no fire on and it was a chilly day and no sign of life.

Just as she turned to walk down the path a voice called to her asking if she was delivering a parcel or mail for Mrs Burns.

"Oh, no, I've actually come to see them. Can you tell me where they are? They never go out, and I'm really shocked to see the house up for sale – is there something wrong with them?"

The neighbour looked at Joanna, asking if she were related or just a friend.

"Well, I suppose I am related in a sort of way."

Not wanting to tell neighbours private business that might embarrass the elderly couple, the little woman in her slippers and apron came a little closer, asking if she would like a cup of tea. She said she would tell her about Mr and Mrs Burns, as she called them, very formally as elderly people did, even though they had known them for years. A quick glance at her watch told Joanna she had plenty of time, and so what if the mail was late? She would claim she had got lost on her new route.

"I'm afraid, my dear," the little woman said, as they sat in her spotlessly clean, warm kitchen with a hot cup of tea steaming on the table, "Mr Burns, Harry, that is, he died, it must be oh, four or five months since."

While Joanna was attempting to digest this shock the kindly soul dropped another bombshell. "And Mrs Burns, Harriet, you know, well, she's in St Mary's rest home on the main road."

"Why?" stuttered Joanna, "Why? I don't understand. I know I haven't been for a while but they were fine. They were managing. I asked them if they needed anything and they said no. I don't understand what could have happened."

"Well, it all started with the men that came to mend the roof. They arrived on a Monday and – do you know? – they were here day after day. Well, I say they were here; they weren't, but there were piles of rubble, sand and stuff, old tiles and buckets of cement, which they left to go hard. A right mess, I can tell you. Anyway, they told old Mr Burns that his roof needed mending. Then I gather from the home help that they told them their chimney stack needed pointing and, oh, lots of other jobs. I tell you, it was never ending; their home help told me that they took old Mr Burns to the bank to draw money out to pay their bill.

"Well, that was the end of him. He took a stroke and never recovered. And poor old Mrs Burns... There, well, she was no good without him. They couldn't hear a word, you know? Both deaf as posts. Well, as far as I know, the house is to be sold to pay for her fees in St Mary's, but she'll not live long without him. Peas in a pod they were; never one without the other, but harmless, you know?"

Joanna was in a state of shock as she drove her van round the rest of her route. She decided that if she hurried up she could call in to St Mary's and see poor old Harriet. She must be in a terrible state without Harry.

As she pushed the buzzer on the large glass door of St Mary's after trying to push it open and finding it locked, she was impatient to be in to find out how Harriet was. Eventually, after several pushes on the buzzer, someone came to let her in. A cleaner, thought Joanna, as she made her way to what looked like an office with a glass door just inside the entrance.

After giving the door a tap, Joanna put her head round as it was very clear that the uniformed person behind the desk was making no move to either answer the door or call her in.

"Excuse me, I wonder if I could see Mrs Burns, Mrs Harriet Burns. I'm a close friend and I didn't know Mr Burns had died and that Mrs Burns, Harriet, was living here now."

"Oh, so you weren't that close a friend, then. Who did you say you were again?" said the uniformed woman, in a stiff no-nonsense manner, with a false smile painted on her face that was obviously used on most occasions in order to appease questioning relatives and elderly patients.

"Actually, they are my little girl's grandparents, and I don't get to see them as often as I would have liked."

Seeing a look in the starchy woman's face that Joanna chose to ignore about Holly's parentage, Joanna carried on, "However, the last time I saw them Mr Burns was fine, as was Harriet. What I don't understand is that my name was on their telephone number chart on their wall, in case of emergencies, yet I was not informed of Harry's death, or that poor Harriet was in a home."

This fell on deaf ears, so to speak, and the officious uniform marched Joanna towards a large room at the end of a very long corridor and pointed to a frail old lady sitting on her own in the corner.

As Joanna moved gradually closer to the elderly lady huddled in a winged high-back chair, she was utterly shocked to see that this poor shell of a woman was Harriet. Her heart stopped and instantly tears clogged her throat and she dashed over to throw her arms around Harriet's pathetically frail, thin, little body. She pulled back in order that Harriet would be able to see what she was saying. Harriet had never been taught to lip read but she was bright enough to know, by the expression you put into your sentences, the drift of what you were saying.

"Harriet, oh, Harriet, I'm so sorry. I missed Harry's funeral. I didn't know, you see?"

Joanna looked at Harriet's face, trying to see if she was understanding any of what she was saying to her. She held her hands and gave them a squeeze to let her know that she was there, but it was increasingly obvious that Harriet wasn't even aware of Joanna's presence. Joanna tried to give her a little shake, tried again to say hello and that it was Joanna come to see her. But there was no response. Joanna gave Harriet another hug, telling her that she wouldn't be a minute, that she was just going to see the nurse and she would be straight back. Not a flicker crossed Harriet's face.

Joanna went back to the office and knocked briefly on the door. Once again, the uniformed lady was sat down, apparently in the action of writing something terribly important, so important that she could not raise her head so that Joanna could request a minute until she was finished.

Joanna was becoming so angered by this bad behaviour that she went straight to the matter that was screaming in her head. "Can you tell me what has happened to Harriet? Why is she not responding to me? Why doesn't she recognise me? Has she had a stroke as well as Mr Burns?"

The uniformed woman looked up with a stare that was meant to freeze a person into submission. But she had met her match in Joanna. As Joel would have said, 'Never mess with a woman on a mission'.

Joanna stood up straight and simply gave back the same look, which took the uniform by surprise. Joanna continued, enquiring, "Matron? Sister?" then waiting for a reply to her question as to what rank she was addressing. The uniform replied, less sure of her ground, saying that she was the manager. However, with no medical title being forthcoming, Joanna doubted very much if she was even a qualified nurse.

Joanna continued in a calm, cool and precise voice. "I asked if you could tell me why Harriet is not responding. Has she suffered a stroke? Is there a medical reason why she is motionless?"

"You're, erm, relative…" This was said with an attitude in her voice that Joanna ignored in order to get to the story. "Harriet could not be kept under control. She would not sit still, and she was flailing her arms around all the time and making terrible noises so she had to be sedated. There is nothing else wrong with her, but you know, of course, she has mental issues?"

"What? Harriet has no mental issues; she is deaf, that's all. You did know she is profoundly deaf, didn't you?"

"My dear, calm yourself. I can assure you everything that can be done is being done for your relative. We have a lot of elderly patients at St Marys and they don't all throw their arms around in order to speak. I'm afraid, for her own good and the safety of the other residents, she had to be sedated. It is all medically approved by our resident doctor."

"Can I ask your rank, Mrs…erm?"

Joanna waited until the uniform gave her a name. If the situation had not been so dire she would have burst out laughing.

"Frost, Mrs Frost, and I am the manager, as I told you earlier."

"However, you are not a trained nurse? Is that right? I don't particularly want to get off on the wrong foot, Mrs Frost." Her very name stuck in Joanna's throat. "But I must tell you that I saw Harry and Harriet less than six months ago; they were both absolutely fine. They are, or rather were, until Harry died, both profoundly deaf, and without signing ability, though they managed their lives quite well and had done ever since they were married.

"I have heard from a neighbour the reason for Harry's stroke, which is that he was being pressured by some fraudsters for money for so-called repairs on their home. But Harriet has all her mental capacity. The reason she throws her arms about, as you term it, is that she attempts without coherent speech to explain her needs. She is not mad. Can you imagine what she must be feeling inside, not being able to communicate with outsiders without Harry there to help?"

Joanna was pink in the face by the time she had got what she wanted to say off her chest to this stiff, starchy uniform.

"Yes, well, Miss, erm, that's as may be. However, I have another sixty residents in St Mary's to consider. I'm sorry about your friend…Harriet, and her husband. However, I'm afraid she is here now. There are no places especially for the deaf, so she will simply have to adapt. However, she is refusing to eat, and if she doesn't eat soon then she will end up in hospital on a drip as we simply can't take responsibility for her. But I can assure you she is receiving the best possible care while she is here. Now, if you will excuse me, I have other patients to deal with."

As the uniform marched away towards the door and the heels of her court shoes clicked on the hard floor Joanna could see her back was rigid with annoyance at such an outburst by a mere relative.

Joanna went back to sit with Harriet, taking her hand in hers, when a woman in an auxiliary's uniform came to her and sat in the vacant seat next to her.

"Hi, I'm Caroline. I work here, and I can see you're upset. I couldn't help but overhear your 'conversation' with Mrs Frost."

This was said with a roll of the eyes from both women.

"Don't worry, she has nothing to do with the care of the patients. Between you and me, she is a pen pusher. I think you must have got a terrible shock when you saw your friend the way she is? But, believe me, she is better now than before she was sedated. She was so unhappy and lost without her husband, who I gather more or less did most of the communicating for them both. Well, she took his death very, very badly, and actually she is much calmer now. For poor Harriet I think it's a better thing.

"I'm not saying I believe in the residents being drugged up to the eyeballs, I don't, but she was so sad and missing her husband so much it was cruel to watch. And, of course, to anyone not knowing that she is unable to speak, it looks strange – she is unaware that the noises she makes are just sounds to everyone else."

Joanna started to explain that Harriet and Harry were fine the last time she had seen them. She told the nice woman with the kindly manner the way in which they were related, including that her daughter was also deaf. That was how she knew what not being able to make herself understood would do to Harriet.

The auxiliary took hold of Joanna's hand, saying in the kindest possible way that Harriet, believe it or not, was happier in her oblivion. "Really, she is. I wouldn't say that if I didn't believe it. And you don't have to worry – there are some lovely, caring staff in St Mary's, despite the appearance Mrs Frost gave. To be honest, if Harriet did slip away through not eating, would it not be a blessing? Yes, sad, but a blessing, because wouldn't she have wanted to go with her husband?"

Joanna could have hugged this kind-hearted woman who seemed to be totally tuned in to the needs of her patients. And as sad as it was horrific seeing Harriet this way, in no way did she want to make her distress at the loss of Harry any worse by insisting to a higher body that her medication be stopped. What good would that do Harriet? She put her arms around her one more time and gave her a hug, whispering in her ear that she wouldn't be forgotten, that Harry was with Kevin, and that, if it was her wish, then soon she would be too. She gave one final squeeze to one of Harriet's frail hands and walked towards the door with tears coursing down her cheeks.

Without a backward glance, she walked out into the late afternoon, which was fast becoming dark. She sat in her little van in the car park and cried her eyes out. Great sobs came from her very soul, for Harry, for Harriet and for Kevin, three lives, three kind souls, and look what life had dealt them. But for the first time soon they would all be together. The car park was the kind of place where no one would ever wonder why someone was crying so desperately; because anyone who had ever visited a friend or relative in such a place knew that the residents were truly 'waiting for God'.

Chapter 20

By the time Joanna pulled the little red van on to the drive it was dark and she felt totally wrung out. She would have to explain to Holly about Grandma and Granddad. It was true that she didn't see them much for a multitude of reasons, which boiled down to communication between them all.

"God, I'm so glad that Holly learned to sign and talk."

Joanna knew that, if it were only that small thing she had ever done for Holly, it was the best and would stand her in good stead for her future.

As they sat at the kitchen table, this was one of the few solemn occasions in their home. On the whole it was a happy house. Joanna explained about Harry and Harriet. Holly came over and gave Joanna a big hug, saying, "Now Granddad is with Daddy they won't be lonely, and when Grandma goes they will all be together so that'll be nice for them, won't it?"

The innocence and simplicity of a child, thought Joanna.

She decided she would go up to bed when the girls did, so, after saying goodnight to Holly, Joanna had a long hot bath where she lingered deep in thought, unable to pull herself out of this pit of depression that threatened to engulf her. But after a good night's sleep and a stern talking to herself, Joanna was once again her optimistic self. And she firmly resolved to do something with her newly gained degree, if only to stop other unsuspecting elderly people falling prey to such locusts. She had no idea what she intended yet, but she would put her mind to it. And when Joanna put her mind to something she usually found a solution.

Things more or less settled down to a domestic pattern once more. It was over a week since she had seen Harriet and she had reasoned with herself that the auxiliary was right; that it would be cruel to drag poor Harriet out of her dream-like existence only to make her nightmare come back, a life without her beloved Harry.

Joanna had finished her new round and would be back on her own on Monday morning. As today was Saturday she had slept a little later when the phone rang. She was having a quick shower before getting dressed and making breakfast. Joel was back at work and Alisha was on days this week, so Joanna was the only one able to answer the phone.

Opening the shower door when she saw the light flashing, she leaned out and grabbed the receiver. She said, "Hello," while spitting the water out of her face and mouth.

"Joanna? Is that you?"

"Yes," Joanna said again while battling with the constant drill of water against her face.

"It doesn't sound like you. Are you all right?"

Suddenly Joanna realised it was Simon's warm voice resonating down the phone line and into her shower with her. She leaned away from the spraying water and, at the same time, attempted to cover herself up as she felt totally off guard speaking to him after all this time, stark naked.

"Yes, yes, sorry, I'm in the shower and there was no one else to answer the phone. I'm fine. Did you need something?"

There was a slight pause at the other end of the phone, after Joanna mentioned she was in the shower, before Simon said, "Oh, it's not important. I'll ring you back when you have…some clothes on."

"No, no, it's fine. Was it something important?, I don't mind."

Simon went on to say, after what sounded like a sharp intake of breath, "Mum and Dad and I were at the hospital the other day. We saw the specialist and Mum was hoping you could call so she can tell you all about it. Unless, of course, you already know from Joel? We bumped into him for a minute or so and he told us about Kevin's parents… Listen, I'm really sorry about them.

"Anyway you must be getting cold now, so just if you get a moment we… Mum and Dad would love you to come. I just thought it's Saturday today… Maybe the girls would come with you? Dad would love to see them."

"Yes, yes, that would be lovely. I would love to hear all about what the consultant said about

William and the girls would love to come. Shall we say one o'clock-ish?"

"Yes, that'll be great. See you soon then, Joanna. Bye."

Joanna replaced the receiver and wrapped herself in a huge bath towel, hugging her body close, thinking of Simon's warm honey-sounding voice that gave her goose bumps. Drat, she thought, now she would have to go through all that again. It was almost like finishing with someone then going back to them – you had to grieve all over again. That was if she could remember that far back to her teenage years.

The girls were totally excited to be going to see William, as they hadn't seen him for a couple of weeks, and Lily, of course, who gave them cake and juice and was ever so nice, the girls thought.

Joanna dressed a little more carefully than usual, as she wouldn't be wearing her work uniform. Joanna couldn't afford a car of her own, though if Joel or Alisha were home she was insured to drive theirs. However, as they were both at work, she and the girls would have to take the little bus.

The girls loved it anyway, because it went all around the houses, something that would annoy most people but that fascinated them. She decided to wear her dark blue denim skirt, which was knee length and flattering on the leg, with a navy vest top tucked inside and a large grey leather belt with a big buckle. Over that she wore a charcoal crop cable cardigan. She put on her best navy tights with no holes in and her dark grey ankle boots. She brushed her hair until it shone and, putting on a little mascara to give her courage, she gave herself one last approving look in the mirror and skipped lightly down the stairs.

The girls both gave each other knowing looks and an exaggerated wink of the eye. Be honest, her innermost thoughts spoke to Joanna: you know you dressed up not only for Simon but also in case Cruella is there, looking all glam even with clothes on this time.

It was a lovely morning, and they enjoyed the mini bus journey, which only took a short time, before they arrived at Simon's gate.

Chapter 21

As the girls ran up the path, the door sprang
instantly open as it always did. However,
instead of Lily standing in the open doorway,
it was Simon. Joanna sighed deeply. She had
dreaded but secretly hoped she would see
Simon. Part of her wanted to run but the other
part wanted to absorb every ounce of him,
drinking in the smell of his aftershave in order
to bottle it for her memory box.

The girls reached him first, puffing a little
from their run from the bus stop, racing to say
hello excitedly to Simon. He patted them both
on the tops of their heads so that they would
see him mouth 'hello' with a huge smile.
Joanna felt almost jealous until something
totally unexpected happened as she walked to
enter: Simon leant down and kissed her cheek.
Joanna was quite flustered; she hadn't
expected that and her face became suffused
with colour.

As they reached the lounge, Lily came straight
to Joanna and kissed her on the cheek like an
old friend. Joanna thought then to herself that
Simon had simply kissed her out of good

manners. She knew families did this; however, she had never known it until she and Holly had gone to live with Joel and Alisha, who hugged and kissed all the time. Part of Joanna was a little disappointed, but all too soon she was hugging Lily back, saying how nice it was to see her.

Joanna burst out, "I've missed you both so much, and so much has happened you won't believe it. Oh, you did get my note, saying I was on a different run but only for a week or so?" queries Joanna.

"Yes," said Lily, "I did. Thank you, dear, that was kind of you."

Then suddenly the conversation stopped as the three adults watched in total amazement as William stood up from his chair, held out his hands and smiled... Actually smiled. The girls took one hand each and asked if they could go for a walk with William. And they walked past all three gaping mouths and out into the yard.

"If I hadn't seen it with my own eyes I wouldn't have believed it. Oh, my dear." Lily started to cry. Great big, fat tears of happiness rolled down her cheeks as she battled to dab them away with her hanky. Joanna was swallowing hard not to cry herself. Although her eyes were very moist, she didn't want to blub in front of Simon. But a quick glance at his face told her that he was fighting his emotions diligently, too.

"Tell me, what did the consultant say?" asked Joanna, excited to hear all the news.

Simon started by saying he had run into Joel at the hospital and that Joel had hoped that his consultant friend, Mr Fortune, would be able to help. "So, obviously, you will tell him how grateful we are for the swift appointment?"

"He was lovely," said Lily. "He chatted to all of us, including William. We told him how much progress he had made since meeting the girls, Holly, in particular, and that they seemed to have a connection with him that no one else could reach.

"He said how interesting that was and asked how much progress he had made previous to meeting the girls. I had to tell him none, that he had sat in that armchair and never moved other than when I almost carried him into the bedroom and the bathroom. I told him," Lily continued, excitedly, "that William was like an empty shell, but now look at him. He can smile, he knows the girls, and he looks forward to seeing them. He really knows and recognises them. I can never thank you and the girls enough, Joanna, never."

Simon continued telling Joanna what Mr Fortune had said. "Because Dad made such good progress once he started, there's no telling how much he could recover. He couldn't guarantee anything or give a prognosis of how much progress he would or could make, but he was very optimistic. He seemed to think that Dad probably had a breakdown, or a series of mini strokes. They gave him a CAT scan and we are still waiting for the results. But he said he would be looking to see if Dad has had a bleed on the brain. If he has, then apparently he is making a good recovery.

"As Mum says, we can never thank you enough, and, of course, Holly, Precious and Joel. Without you all, Dad could have sat there until he died."

Lily nipped out to the kitchen to bring the tray in with coffee for the grown-ups and juice for the girls. She bustled out, telling them to sit down, for goodness sake; they looked as though there weren't any seats. And it wouldn't take her a minute. Joanna sat down and suddenly felt a little shy – the girls outside and Lily in the kitchen left Simon and Joanna alone for the first time since they were in Scotland.

"I hope you didn't mind taking the car back? I'm afraid I got caught up in something important," said Simon, a little shyly, thought Joanna.

"I've missed seeing you and…erm… So have Mum and Dad, of course. I've missed seeing the girls, too. They are a tonic for anyone, and Dad genuinely feels a real affinity with them.

"I was very sorry to hear about Kevin's parents; Joel told me briefly when we met at the hospital. I can't begin to know how you must have been feeling. I wish I could have been there to help you," Simon said with real concern in his deep voice. "It has to have been the same shameless lot that would have without doubt done the same to my parents, had we not had the good fortune to meet you."

Leaning over he laid his large, tanned hand on Joanna's for a split second, giving it a brief squeeze. "So I take back what I said when you leapt out of the woodshed on top of me."

This was said in an attempt to lighten the mood again. Joanna, not sure what to say next, could have bitten her tongue off, for what came out of her mouth was, "And how is Lydia? Is she still here with you?"

Simon said that yes, Lydia was still here, although she had just nipped down to the chemist for something or other and wouldn't be long. Just then, the girls arrived back indoors with William and walked him back to his chair, where he dutifully sat down like a well-behaved child without a murmur, but with a serene smile fixed on his gentle face.

The girls rushed to Simon, asking excitedly whether he was going to bring bags and shoes and clothes in his planes when his business started.

"No, I'm sorry, girls, I won't be bringing in anything as exciting as that, I'm afraid. I will be transporting machine parts and packages and all sorts of boring things like that."

"Oh, the lady outside on the telephone said you would be bringing in bags and packages, and when you start the business up properly she could supply them regularly."

"Who said that, Holly?" said Simon in a firm but gentle tone.

Precious and Holly both signed and spoke at the same time. "The angry lady outside, on her mobile phone. She said she would be able to get a regular supply of stuff, you know, bags and things."

Simon bent down to the girls' level and smiled, asking the girls to tell him exactly what they had seen, saying that he would be very interested and maybe he would even take them to McDonalds as a treat, though possibly not today. He patted the seat next to him, suggesting that they sat down and told him everything.

"Well," said Holly, "Precious and William and me were sat on the seat round the back next to the lady's car and she came out and she was very angry. We didn't touch her car, honestly, but her face was very angry. She was arguing with someone on her phone. She was asking directions, I think, because she said she needed a bag and that soon she would have lots of bags when the business was started."

Precious took up the story, saying, "William and Lily are going to live in a home when the business starts because she will be with you. Is it a nice home, Simon, where William's going? We will miss him so much, and you, and Lily, we will miss you all. I wish you weren't leaving."

"Don't worry, girls, William and Lily will be with me and it's a lovely house. Ask your mum – she has seen it and she liked it. And you are both welcome to visit any time, I promise. And thank you for telling me what the lady said. The next time I see you, will you let me take you to McDonalds and buy you a happy meal? And, as a treat from William and Lily, you can buy something off the barrows, how's that?"

"Oh, wow, yes, oh, thank you so much." The girls knelt down on the floor next to William, drinking juice and eating their favourite home-made biscuits that Lily always made. Simon seemed lost in deep thought.

Just then, a throaty roar from a car engine sped out of the drive, which Joanna gathered must be Lydia's car leaving. Relieved at the thought of not having to face her, she relaxed into her seat a little more, taking a drink of her coffee.

Simon looked very thoughtful. Whatever it was that the girls had seen, he was definitely giving it some consideration. The girls were showing William pictures out of the book of villages again, which they were sure he enjoyed, and Lily was asking Joanna what Scotland had been like.

Lily was watching Simon. When he left the room for a minute, Lily whispered to Joanna, "There's something funny about that woman. I don't think she is Simon's girlfriend. Well, they don't act like it, and she is as jumpy as a cat on a hot tin roof. If you ask me, there is something wrong with her and Simon is too well mannered to send her away, take my word for it…"

Just then, Simon came back in with an envelope in his hand, saying to Joanna, "Would you give this to Joel, with my and my parents' gratitude? Tell him to have a wonderful time."

This cryptic sentence was said with a smile on his face, yet Joanna could tell that what the girls had told him had distracted him. Simon suddenly asked how they had travelled, and where was their car?

"We came by bus, and actually we should be leaving now, but I'm back on my normal route next week so I will see you then. Come on, girls," Joanna said, tapping the girls on the shoulder. "Say goodbye to William and Lily. We should be getting back now, I'm the cook tonight."

The girls pretended to groan at the thought of Joanna cooking but they were laughing to show they were only kidding. They said their goodbyes to William.

"Don't you have a car Joanna?" Simon asked.

"No, I can't afford one. Normally, either Alisha's or Joel's car would be there, so I can use one of theirs, but they are both at work today so we took the bus. The girls love the bus and I don't mind at all."

"I'm sorry, I wouldn't have asked you to come if I had known you had no car. You must let me get you a taxi; I haven't bothered hiring another car as we have had Lydia's to run around in while we have been looking at planes this week," Simon said, looking concerned at the thought of them getting public transport.

"No, no, honestly, the girls would be disappointed. They really do love the bus. Between you and me, they watch all the people and see what they are talking about and what they are all wearing. They are becoming very fashion conscious, if you remember."

Just then the phone rang, and, as the little group walked towards the door, Lily went to answer it. While they were saying their goodbyes, Lily shouted that it was for Simon. He bent down and gave each of the girls a kiss on the cheek with a lovely smile, saying that he wouldn't forget his promise and that he would see them soon. The girls were all smiles at the thought of their forthcoming treat. Then Simon leant down to Joanna and kissed her on the cheek, saying softly that he would see her very soon. As he dashed off to answer the phone, Lily waved from the door while Joanna and the girls wandered down the road towards the bus stop.

The girls skipped and talked to each other, discussing what they would buy and how they couldn't wait to see Simon again and what a lovely time they would have. Turning to Joanna, who was in a pensive daydream, they chorused excitedly, "When do you think it will be, Mummy?"

The girls took one look at Joanna and gave each other one of their winks, telling each other in silent sign to look at Joanna's face. The dreamy expression she wore and the fact that she was deep in thought… Both girls attempted to smother their giggles, knowing for sure whom she would be thinking about.

Chapter 22

When they arrived home Alisha's car was already in the drive. Joanna was glad she had prepared the evening meal; otherwise Alisha would have had to start cooking after a long, hard shift. As the girls ran into the house like a herd of elephants, Alisha shouted, "Hello," to Joanna, saying that she was in the lounge with her tired old feet up.

"Hi, where have you all been, then?" Alisha asked.

"We have been to see William, Lily and Simon," said Precious, "and Simon is taking us for a treat soon. We don't know when; he is going to let Joanna know. He said McDonalds and something from the barrows at the mall, yippee."

"Phew," said Alisha to them both. "And what on earth did you do to deserve that, you noisy little horrors?"

A quick shrug of their shoulders and off they went upstairs to talk about girls' stuff and what on earth they would buy off the barrows this time.

"Hi, you had a hard shift, you look exhausted," Joanna told Alisha. "Do you want a coffee, or something stronger?"

"Oh, just a long, tall glass of fruit juice, please; it was so hot on the ward. I feel so drained, you know, I could sleep on a clothes line. So was Cruella there? Did she have clothes on this time?"

"Yes, she was there. Well, I say that, but I didn't actually see her, thank goodness for that. The girls did, though, and yes, I presume she had clothes on as she went out in her car. Oh, by the way, Simon gave me this for Joel," Joanna said, handing the stiff white envelope to Alisha. "He said to have a 'wonderful time', whatever that's all about."

Alisha naturally opened the envelope, as all wives do with their husband's mail, and with a sharp intake of breath she looked up to Joanna, asking, "Did he tell you what was in it?"

"No."

Alisha handed Joanna the contents of the envelope, which turned out to be three tickets to Barbados with an open date on, allowing travel dates to be confirmed. Attached was a little note from Simon, saying, 'Thank you for all your help, S.W.'

"Oh, wow, oh, wow, Alisha! How wonderful! Oh, just think… You will be able to visit all your family; oh my God, that's fabulous."

Alisha had jumped off the sofa, tired feet soon forgotten as she and Joanna danced around the room.

"Wait until Joel sees these. Oh, gosh, we will have to try to arrange holiday cover. Oh, I hope we can; it's always difficult to get holiday time together."

"You will get time off," said Joanna firmly. "You are entitled to it. How many shifts have you covered for others and how many has Joel done in a row until he could hardly speak he was so tired? You are putting in your holiday forms and you are going, all three of you!"

"Oh, Joanna, I can't believe it. We have never had anything given to us. Isn't this so kind of Simon? After all, we haven't done anything, unlike you. Oh, goodness only knows what he has in store for you, my girl," Alisha said in her best Caribbean drawl, insinuating something intimate between Simon and Joanna.

"Don't be silly. I've had my holiday in Scotland and I wouldn't change that for the world. I hope you have the most wonderful holiday – you both deserve it."

"So tell me all about Cruella then. She seems very quiet."

"Well, actually, I don't really know what it was all about, but she certainly wasn't quiet, according to the girls." Joanna told Alisha about what the girls had said to Simon about Lydia, and how she had said that when the business was up and running they would be hauling bags and she would have a regular supply, or whatever.

"But Simon says he isn't doing clothes, which I thought was a bit unlikely anyway," she continued. "Whatever it was, he took them very seriously. The girls said she was very angry and appeared to be having an argument on her mobile with someone and getting instructions on where to meet them. But Simon had said she was nipping out to the chemist. And Lily said," Joanna mimicked in a cartoon-like conspirator voice, "she didn't trust her and that there was something wrong with her. She waited until Simon had left the room then more or less whispered that she thought there was something wrong with her."

"What – ill you mean?"

"I don't know, I'm not sure. Yes, I think so, but Lily couldn't tell me any more than that, because Simon came back into the room. Except she didn't think they were dating as in 'girl and boy type thing, you know?' she said, bless her."

"Oh, I wonder how she found that out. You must tell me more, girl. You have to keep your ears and eyes open when you go on Monday. This sounds interesting. I bet you she wasn't talking about handbags either; it sounds like drugs or something like that to me."

"No, no, don't be silly, you're imagining things. You've worked in Casualty too long – you have become a cynic. Good grief, woman, look at us – we are slandering Cruella's 'bad' name here, ha ha. Sit down and rest your poor feet until Joel comes in, because no doubt you will be dancing about again when he sees those tickets."

"You are too innocent, Joanna. Mark my words, when there is whispering and strange behaviour there are usually drugs at the bottom of it. I should know, I see it all the time, and I don't just mean patients. The staff are almost as bad."

"Surely not – Simon wouldn't have a partner who wasn't on the up and up. I know that much in the short time I've known him. This is his dream business – he wouldn't take the risk. I'm sure there is another explanation."

"You mark my words," Alisha advised. You said Lily thought there was something wrong with her, enough to sound worried. Well, a mother isn't very often far from the mark."

"Well, whatever it is, Simon must be on to it; he seemed very interested in what the girls had to say. Right, let's get the supper on the go before Joel gets in and starts dancing."

As predicted Joel was like a man with two heads. He swung Alisha around, doing some sort of wild Caribbean dance, Precious and Holly were imitating the dance, and everyone was clapping their hands so the girls knew that they were singing, although they could only imagine what it sounded like, which was pretty bad, to be honest. But they all danced until they were exhausted, feeling happier than they had been for a long time, thanks to Simon's generosity.

Chapter 23

Joanna didn't see Lily and William, or Simon, for a whole week. She was asked to work in the depot, sorting mail, to replace a colleague who was on sick leave. Joanna thought to herself that a few months ago this wouldn't have bothered her at all. This was normal practice and sometimes she enjoyed the change. However, now that she had something to look forward to each day she wasn't so keen. She enjoyed so much seeing Lily, William, and – who was she kidding? – she desperately wanted her daily fix of Simon's handsome face. At last, the week was over and she was back to her normal round.

As the new week started, Joanna began her round, trying to quell her excitement at seeing Simon again. It was pitch dark and it was obvious that there had been a hard overnight frost as winter fast approached. She drove with care and much slower than normal, so it was slightly later by the time she reached the old station. Joanna pulled the van up and sat for a moment, slightly stunned at what she saw, although she didn't know why she should be. It had been only a matter of time. There attached to the gatepost was the brightly coloured For Sale sign.

As the front door popped open like magic as usual, another shock was to see Lily holding her stick up in the air, indicating the lack of her hulking great plaster cast. With a wide smile on her face, she came slowly towards Joanna to show how well she could walk once again.

"Oh, that's brilliant, Lily. I bet you feel so much better to be rid of that horrible thing," said Joanna.

"Oh, you have no idea – just to get into the bath instead of having to have a shower with a plastic bag over my cast. Last night I had the most glorious bath once I'd put William to bed. It was sheer heaven.

"Come in, dear, come in. The coffee's ready; I'll just boil the kettle again. Your replacement postman said you were working in the depot last week and we all really missed you. But first I must show you this."

Lily bustled them into the lounge. Instead of William sitting in his usual chair by the fire, the chair had been moved to the window, which allowed William to look outside and see who was coming.

"Simon moved his chair to the window and you won't believe this but he saw you coming. He did: he turned to me and, when I looked out, there you were. I can't believe the amount of progress he has made. Oh, Joanna, I'm so happy to see his face light up again and know there is something in there and that he actually recognises me and Simon, and, of course, you and especially the girls. He loves to see the girls.

"Simon's had to go back to Gatwick for a few days, but he said he was going to ring you. Some sort of business, I'm not sure what, but he will only be away a couple of days, he said."

Joanna tried not to let Lily see her disappointment, but inside her heart sank to her feet when she heard Simon wasn't at home. It seemed ages since that fleeting kiss on her cheek the day she had brought the girls on the bus. But she tried to tell herself that he was going to ring her, so that was something to look forward to. God, she thought, I'm like a schoolgirl with a crush.

As Joanna left, giving a wave to William at the window and Lily at the door, she could almost see a response from William. She couldn't help but be pleased for them both, despite the fact that, deep down in the pit of her stomach, she was feeling… What was she feeling? Joanna sat in a lay-by on one of the local beauty high spots and looked down over Derby as she examined her emotions.

Tears clogged her throat as she admitted the truth to herself. She had broken her golden rule, the one she had made when she was a child being passed from one foster home to another; giving everything she could possibly give to each potential new parent only to be passed on for one reason or another.

She had vowed then, as young as she was, never to give her heart and soul to anyone ever again until she was absolutely positive that they wouldn't break it. Yet here she was again. She knew now that she loved Simon; it wasn't simply a crush, as she had kept telling herself. She didn't know how or when, and she realised she was mad after only knowing him a matter of a month or so. But some things you just knew.

What would she do when they moved? Joanna couldn't bear to think about it; but one thing she did know was that she couldn't simply go on in her job, nothing changing from day to day. She had loved her job, and they had been wonderful, had supported her when her need was the greatest. She knew now, though, that, no matter what happened in the future, she wanted to speak for those people who had nobody else to speak for them. If that meant working part-time and doing something from home, she would do it. She had to have a plan for the future or she knew she would pine away. She remembered that feeling all too well from her childhood.

It was later in the week when Alisha answered the phone while they were eating their evening meal, then said, "It's Simon for you, Joanna."

This was said in the kind of tone that everyone could see was suggestive by her actions. The girls giggled and turned to watch Joanna's mouth as she spoke, until Joel tapped them both on their hands. "Hey, you two, it is rude to listen in on people's private conversations."

This said, it was obvious to the girls that he, too, was listening to every word, and the girls puffed out their cheeks in annoyance. When the conversation had ended, Joanna's spirits were visibly lifted and she had a grin from ear to ear. Alisha and Joel gave each other knowing looks while waiting to hear what she was going to tell the girls, as it had clearly involved them, judging by the snippets they had overheard.

"Who would like to go…to a bonfire display on Saturday?"

The girls screamed together as they always did when they were excited. "We do, we do! With Simon?"

"Yes, with Simon. He is going to pick us up at five o'clock and he said to tell you to wrap up warm."

"Yeah, yeah," the girls chorused as Joanna sat back down at the table. She explained that Simon had been back to Gatwick for some mysterious reason and that he had hired a car to drive home this time. Alisha gave another wink and a knowing nod to Joel, who simply couldn't keep it discreet and said, in his most outrageous Caribbean drawl, "Are you happier now, my little chickadee? Now that Simon is home?"

"Joel, don't embarrass the girl," Alisha remonstrated, kicking Joel's leg under the table. Joel shrugged his shoulders, pretending he didn't know what he had said that was wrong.

Joanna flushed bright red and attempted to say that she was perfectly fine and didn't know what they meant. But nothing could take the smile from Joanna's face all evening.

Bonfire night arrived and the girls attempted their out of tune version of 'Remember, remember the fifth of November' as they were so excited. They had never been allowed out on Guy Fawkes' night before, for the most obvious reason that they would not be able to hear if a firework was to explode next to them. However, as this was an organised display and there would be two adults to supervise the girls, Alisha and Joel agreed. They didn't want to be killjoys, even though they had both seen the consequences of the careless use of fireworks in their jobs.

The girls were all wrapped up with hats, gloves and wellington boots, as was Joanna. This wasn't a fashion parade, she chided herself when she was dressing. She still wanted to look attractive, though – when her nose went red with the cold, as it always did, she didn't want it to clash with her sweater.

She decided to wear her fleece-lined duffle coat, which almost reached her knees, with a cream polo jumper up to her ears so that she didn't need a scarf. Her denims were her warmest pants and she also wore her wellingtons, which she had for when she got stuck in the snow while at work. She simply refused to wear a hat as it made her look about ten years old.

The girls were very excited and watched outside for Simon coming, so Joanna didn't need to look out, too. The girls' voices shouted from the rooftops when he arrived.

He jumped out of the car looking larger than life, as he always did. Suddenly, thought Joanna, the world was a bigger place. When Simon was here, everything changed – her mood, the children's moods. Oh, what would she do when he wasn't here? Joanna shook herself vigorously forcing herself to forget it. Until it actually happened, she would pretend it never would.

As he opened the back door for the girls and the front for Joanna, he leant down and kissed her once again, softly, fleetingly on the cheek. But Joanna was sure this couldn't simply be a greeting, or could it? The girls had not missed the tender kiss and rolled their lips together as if to say their lips were sealed until they could talk privately later.

Alisha and Joel waved them off, but the girls couldn't have been more excited if they had tried and hardly even looked back. Simon turned to the girls in the back seat, asking them if they were looking forward to it, and he pulled back theatrically to cover his ears for the noisy response, which by now he had come to expect from them. "I take it that's a yes, then?

"Hi." He leaned towards Joanna and looked into her eyes, not giving her time to hide her thoughts, even if she had wanted to, when he asked, "Have you missed me? I'm sorry I had to dash back to Gatwick. I had a little unfinished business to deal with. Are you okay?"

"Yes, I'm fine, and…erm…yes, I did miss you." She coughed suddenly, saying, "And your parents," in an effort to cover her mistaken outburst.

Joanna thought to herself, once again you have broken your golden rule, you've told him you missed him. But Joanna simply couldn't help herself. And, on this occasion, Simon's look seemed to say that he had missed her, too. Still, Joanna had learned over the years not to trust looks.

Simon and Joanna took hold of the girls' hands so that they wouldn't for a moment become separated from them. Simon looked after all of them like a natural father. Soon the fireworks were lighting up the sky to squeals of delight from the crowds. The girls were jubilant and jumped up and down with delight, though it would've seemed a sad thing to a hearing person who realised that the display was set to the most wonderful, stirring music, meaning that it was something the girls would never be able to appreciate.

A quick look at Simon and she could see that he had, at that moment, had the same thought. As he looked into Joanna's eyes in the lit-up sky he could see the raw emotion that the girls' deafness still, after all this time, caused. He put his arm around Joanna's shoulders and drew her towards him, giving her a comforting hug, and they both smiled through misty eyes.

The girls were totally exuberant and loved every moment. When the night began coming to an end, Simon slipped away and bought hot dogs for everyone, which tasted like ambrosia to them all in the cold night air. As the crowds started to disperse and they made their way to the exit, the girls gave each other knowing looks with big eyes and swallowed smiles as they had seen Simon's arm around Joanna's shoulders. They, it would seem, were almost as happy as Joanna herself at his action.

They reached the gates that exited the field and Simon saw a toffee apple stand that he simply couldn't resist. They walked slowly back towards the car park, enjoying the evening, which didn't seem quite so cold any more. The smell of sulphur in the air from the fireworks gave the evening a magical atmosphere. They chatted as they leisurely chewed on their toffee apples.

As they drove home and the girls chatted to each other in the back, Joanna didn't know why she had to torture herself, but she did. Telling Simon she couldn't help but notice the For Sale sign on the station, she asked if he had had any interest, hoping the reply would be not yet.

To her absolute horror, though, Simon said, "Oh yes, actually we haven't had a viewing yet, but apparently the estate agent himself is interested. I have also put in an offer for the Oban field and it has been accepted. This is the worrying part, as it has to happen more or less simultaneously, because I've taken a bridging loan for a week or two until my house goes through quite quickly, I hope. I've laid out a very large amount of cash, as I've just purchased two planes, as well." This was said with a flourish by Simon.

"Oh, wow, really?" Joanna's voice was a mixture of pleasure, envy and sadness, and she had to be very careful not to let it show, because she knew that would be so unfair as this was Simon's dream.

"I know this won't mean anything to you but I have managed to buy a six seater plus cargo space King Air 350 from an ex-buddy of mine I knew in the RAF. He's upgrading, so I know it's in very good order. And I have bought a ten-year-old Cessna Astra SPX – it's a beauty. I'm more or less hoping for things to be on the move by the end of December or the beginning of January. I can't believe it, I am like a child with excitement. To be honest, I've never been this happy for a long time."

As Simon said how happy he was, he reached over and put his hand on Joanna's knee, giving her a look that she couldn't fathom. She was determined not to be a spoilsport and let Simon's news spoil his pleasure, and their wonderful evening. And as they pulled on to the drive Joanna said she had been told by Joel that Simon must come in for coffee or he would want to know the reason why.

So the loud, excited foursome burst into the peaceful scene of Alisha and Joel snuggled up on the sofa. The children both spoke together, shouting from the front door as they kicked their wellington boots off. Telling all about the fireworks and hotdogs, and the toffee apples, they burst into fits of giggles as they said that Simon had had to keep Joanna warm by cuddling her all night. Then the girls ran excitedly into the lounge.

Joanna, unable to face Simon, suddenly looked down while taking her boots off so that he wouldn't see how embarrassed she was. Trust those little horrors, she thought; she'd kill them later. But Simon suddenly lifted her face and gave her a brief but warm kiss on her lips, and one of his gorgeous smiles, which said she had no need to be embarrassed as he wasn't.

Joel greeted Simon in his warm, friendly way, taking his hand and shaking it profusely, saying he couldn't thank him enough for the airline tickets. Simon, however, brushed his generosity aside, saying simply that it was a perk of his job and that they were very welcome.

Joanna went into the kitchen to help Alisha with the coffee tray and the girls disappeared upstairs to get ready for bed as Alisha had told them it was grown-up time now. The girls went without another murmur, knowing they had had a wonderful treat and not to push it.

"How was your night then?" smiled Alisha in that 'tell me all' way.

"It was wonderful and the girls loved it."

"And you? Did you love it?"

"Yes," said Joanna, knowing Alisha wanted more… More information.

"Well, the girls said he cuddled you all night – did he? Did he kiss you?"

Joanna was trying not to get all embarrassed again and said tentatively that yes he had put his arm around her shoulders and yes he had kissed her briefly.

"But, Alisha, he is going to move soon. He has bought the airfield and he has just bought two planes, the station almost has a buyer, and he hopes to be gone by Christmas, so what good is there in dwelling on the occasional kiss?"

"This is a good man, Joanna, my girl, take my word for it. He wouldn't lead you on for no reason, I'm positive. I feel it in my bones, girl. Now come on, bring the tray and think positive."

As the women entered the room it was clear that Simon and Joel had been talking about something quite serious. This made a change for Joel, who usually found it impossible to be serious when it didn't involve work. As they all sat down and started drinking their coffee, Joanna noticed there was definitely an air of mystery.

"What? What?" Joanna asked everyone. "What's happening? It's not my birthday – that's usually when the conversation goes quiet when people are talking about you. What is it? Spit it out, all of you!"

"Well, Joanna…" started Joel in his exaggerated Caribbean drawl, which he did when he was procrastinating.

"Yes?"

"What Joel is trying to tell you is that we have managed to get time off together so that we can take our trip to Barbados."

"Well, that's wonderful, but why all the strange looks?"

"Because…" said Joel and Alisha together, "it will be over Christmas and we have never been parted for a Christmas since we moved in together. You see, they are going to cover with a skeleton staff, and would you believe they said yes when we told them of our plans? But we feel terrible about leaving you and Holly alone at Christmas."

Before Joanna could say a word, Simon cut in firmly, saying that they wouldn't be alone. They would be spending Christmas with him and his parents.

"Listen, if you let me get a word in, I think it's wonderful that you can take time off and I am really, really pleased for you all. You deserve it, and thanks to Simon's tickets you can go, so stop thinking about others. I will have a wonderful time and so will Holly."

"Are you sure, Joanna? We feel awful and we simply won't go if we thought you would be unhappy."

"Rubbish! You will go and Holly and I will be fine, I won't hear another thing about it. The only thing that worries me, though…" she said to the three faces waiting to see if they could solve the problem. "Joel will be unbearable when he comes back. His accent will be unintelligible once he meets up with his relatives."

They all laughed and agreed with what Joanna had said.

The rest of the evening passed with talk of golden sands and warm breezes compared to cold winter nights and frost on the car in the mornings.

Simon stood to go and Joanna saw him to the door to thank him for a wonderful night, telling him that the girls had loved every moment of it, even though she needn't have bothered as he was never in any doubt that they had loved it.

Taking hold of Joanna's hands, he said he had enjoyed it every bit as much as they had. It made everything so much better, he said, being part of a family.

"And you? Did you have a good time?" On saying this, Simon moved in closer to Joanna, slipping one arm around her waist and tipping her chin up with his other warm hand, so that he could see into her eyes.

"Yes, I had a lovely time." Joanna breathed deeply in the curve of his arm, wishing this night would never end.

"I mean it, about Christmas. You can decide if you want to spend Christmas Eve here with Holly and come to us for Christmas Day, but whichever way it is you are coming. We want you too; it would make us all so happy to spend Christmas together."

As Joanna looked into his eyes shyly she could see something – she wasn't sure what – and the next moment she was incapable of coherent thought as his mouth pressed firmly on her lips, pressing and caressing them tenderly but firmly. The strength left her knees and she found herself almost being held by his firm arm around her waist.

He whispered in her ear before letting her go, "Promise. Promise me that you and Holly will be with us for Christmas."

And Joanna whispered back, through lips that felt numb from his kisses, that yes, yes, she would promise. With that he gently pushed her inside, saying it was cold and she should go in. Joanna watched as he pulled out of the drive and off into the darkness.

Chapter 24

Part of Joanna felt uplifted by Simon's continued interest in her and Holly's lives. The other half tried not to think too deeply about it. She didn't want Holly to be hurt when he moved up to Scotland. Holly had become really fond of Simon, as indeed had the whole family.

A pattern began where Simon either called at the house, or Joanna and the girls went to see him and his parents. The change in William was uncanny. Since sitting at the window he had begun to shuffle about in his chair when anyone came up the drive, and when he saw Joanna's van he would actually stand up as if he was going to answer the door.

There was definitely a smile now, and when Joanna took his hand he would grip it, letting her know he was pleased to see her. Joanna didn't always see Simon when she called for coffee during the day, as the new business seemed to be going full steam ahead. Lily told Joanna that the estate agent had indeed bought the station, but that Simon had said that he wouldn't be leaving until after the New Year.

The moving van was booked for the second of January.

That date seemed to drop like a stone into Joanna's lap and all day that's all she could think about. Yet, for some strange reason, it didn't seem to be bothering anyone else. Alisha and Joel were positive that Simon must have a master plan. They were absolutely smitten with him, as were the girls.

Joanna had seen things like this before when she was a child and had hoped that her current foster parents were definitely going to keep her, as she had been so good and they seemed to like her a lot, only to be disappointed at the last minute; and, for no good reason that she could see, she was moved on.

She and Holly decided that they would spend Christmas Eve in their own home and Christmas Day with Simon and his parents. Alisha and Joel could talk about nothing else but their trip now that they could genuinely see that it really didn't upset Joanna. Alisha was trying to buy summer clothes in the middle of winter but Joel didn't care as long as he had his Hawaiian long shorts with the large flowers on, which he assured them were standard dress over there.

Christmas grew ever closer. Simon phoned one Saturday to ask if Joanna and the girls would like to go to the mall Christmas shopping before the crowds got any worse. This news was met with the usual mayhem from the girls.

He said he would pick them up at eleven the next day. So, on the Friday night, the girls sat at the kitchen table writing out lists of what they were going to buy for whom. Joel had been instructed to hand over Precious's pocket money, as had Joanna with Holly's. Joel said they looked more like miniature Fagins, the pair of them counting out their money like professionals.

When Simon arrived, he found the girls standing on the doorstep waiting for him. Later, he joked with Joanna that these girls weren't normal – no women were ever ready before him. When they saw how busy the mall was, Joanna gave the girls their usual lecture before they got out of the car. They hadn't to wander off – if they wanted to see a different shop then they must wait and they would all go.

Simon was totally impressed at how the girls solemnly promised. As he had been out with them several times now, he knew without a shadow of a doubt that they would without question follow Joanna's instructions. It didn't bear thinking about what would happen if one of them became separated.

The mall was a winter wonderland of colour and probably had been since the middle of September. The girls didn't know where to look first – huge Christmas trees were suspended from the rafters, massive baubles of deep Christmas red hung from great swathes of white imitation ferns that told us it was Christmas, apparently. Christmas carols played continuously throughout the mall, which was the only part of the experience the girls were missing out on. However, they were so excited about the visual array of baubles and tinsel that they had no idea that they were missing out on the musical experience.

While the area was clear, they let the girls look in the shop windows. When it became a little more crowded, they each took hold of one of the girl's hands, which worked very well.

After two hours of buying and browsing, Simon said he was in need of a sugar break and could they stop for coffee and cakes? To the girls this sounded like heaven, so they found an outdoor café and Simon went to the counter with Holly while Precious sat with Joanna. When they returned with a tray laden with the most calorific selection of delicious cakes, Joanna could almost feel the waistband of her skirt tightening.

While they had been waiting at the table, Joanna had spotted a shop she would like to go into, but, as it was a surprise for Simon, she suggested he watch the girls for two minutes and she would dash over.

"And I hope you will leave me a piece of that delicious coffee cake, if you can possibly manage without it," Joanna said sarcastically.

Joanna knew exactly what she wanted and it took only minutes to order as the company delivered them to your home after they had been embroidered. She hadn't known what on earth she could buy a person like Simon so she had settled on a black sweatshirt and two polo shirts with the logo specially printed on. 'Simon Winter Cargo & Courier Service' printed in gold thread.

She was back within two minutes minus any parcels, which went unnoticed by the girls who were ticking items off their lists.

Replenished and ready to start over, they shopped non-stop for two more hours before everyone declared that they had completed their lists and were again hungry.

Joanna thought this was just about the bravest thing Simon had done for the girls. Not only was it Saturday but the McDonalds was absolutely heaving with Christmas shoppers. Still, he bravely battled to the counter, coming back with a tray full of meals and shakes.

"I think you deserve a medal, do you know that? I think I should buy you one for Christmas. I can't believe it – either you are a masochist or you are dead from the neck up. Not only to come to McDonalds for a second time on a Saturday but in the run-up to

Christmas… Well, my hat is off to you."
Joanna pretended to lift her hat to him, and
Simon laughed, saying he didn't mind.

"Actually," he said so that only she would
hear, which wasn't difficult given the din of
children shouting, "I'm getting in practice for
when I have to do it with my own children."

Joanna's heart leapt. She didn't know quite
what to make of that but his eyes were smiling.
She gave an automatic laugh, as you do when
you don't know what to say, and left it there.

They eventually wound their way back to the
car. Poor Simon appeared to be carrying the
bulk of the parcels, although the girls were
hanging on tightly to the ones they had chosen
as their treat from Simon from the barrows.

Joanna was very proud that the girls hadn't
even hinted to Simon about their treats, which
he had promised them along with their
McDonalds. They considered that they had
been lucky enough for one day. But as they
came across the same barrow as they had been
to last time, where there was a seat to sit down
on while they chose their purchases, Simon

knew from last time that this could be a lengthy process. Looking to Joanna to see how much he was allowed to give them, it was decided that three pounds was more than enough or they would get spoiled.

As they sat down with all their parcels, Simon and Joanna looked at each other and laughed out loud. They were totally exhausted, yet the girls were full of beans.

"Do you know, Joanna, I see children at the airport, in England, and abroad, and I have seen such a change in the behaviour of children since I was young. And, to be honest, I was beginning to think children with manners were a thing of the past. Since meeting Holly and Precious I know how wrong I was. But it must have been even harder for you, Joel and Alisha. The temptation to spoil a child with a disability must be overwhelming, to give them more than you should for their sake. And, yet, you have all found this balance, which has produced such lovely children that you have restored my faith in the modern family again."

Normally Joanna would have shushed any talk of special children, but she could relate to what Simon said. "I agree, actually. I see children who, if they were mine, I would ground for a month until they learned manners. And yes, it is really hard not to give just that little bit more because of their disability. But I think Joel and Alisha would say the same as me, that we, most of the time, forget that the girls have a disability. We treat them with respect and we hope they will treat us the same. We suggest an alternative rather than simply saying no, and we discuss any large issues and hope to come to an agreement, which we usually do."

They watched the girls as they bartered with the little, plump woman on the stall and eventually they parted with their money in exchange for a paper bag of goodies.

"Please can we go back to the car now before I drop with exhaustion?" Simon pretended to almost fall under the weight of his carrier bags, and the girls took pity on him and Joanna, saying they were ready to go home now.

On the drive home, Joanna had the kind of fuzzy feeling you have when you are really happy. All thoughts of Simon moving away were pushed firmly to the back of her head until at least the end of December she had decided.

Simon seemed deep in thought, as did Joanna, and the girls decided to play spot the Christmas trees in people's windows as they drove past.

They pulled into the drive, then Joanna spotted something leaning against the garage. She said to nobody in particular, "Uh-oh."

"What?" Simon queried her comment.

"I spot the next Christmas ritual. If I were you I'd make a run for it, quick."

"Why?"

Joanna indicated the large, fresh pine tree that was leaning precariously against the garage door. It would seem that the girls spotted it at the same time, as they screamed in unison, "Christmas tree, yeah, yeah!"

"Oh my God, I'll kill whichever one it was who decided to buy that thing today."

"Oh, but putting the Christmas tree up is a wonderful time."

"Well, it may be, but after a day's shopping?" Joanna feigned disinterest.

After they all clambered out of the car, the girls ran in to make sure that the tree was going to be put up tonight. They ran back to Simon, who was about to drop off the parcels and go, and grabbed one of his hands each, saying he must come and help them.

"You must, Simon, please. Please," both girls said pleadingly. Simon gave Joanna a questioning look.

"If you have any energy left and don't want to escape then you are more than welcome. In fact, I am pleading with you because I am going to put my feet up and watch."

They went in to eat the wonderful meal that they could smell from the front door. Alisha had cooked it; which was just as well, as, if they had eaten one of Joel's specials, nobody

314

would have had the energy left to put up a Christmas tree. It was left to Joel and Simon to fit the stand on to the tree while the girls sorted out all the decorations that they had accumulated over the years.

Some of the decorations didn't bear scrutiny, as the girls had made them at school, but were kept simply out of tradition. There was the squinty-eyed snowman that Alisha had knitted and the papier mâché stars and shapes that the girls had made and painted in ghoulish colours. The fairy had fallen off so many times she was rather tatty now and her head kept falling off. She had been superseded by a much larger, fancier fairy, but no one had the heart to throw the old one away so they both went on the tree.

Alisha and Joanna both flopped out on the sofa with a glass of well-earned wine in their hands, watching in amusement as the four gradually covered the once nude Christmas tree until not a square inch of pine was left. When they decided the job was done, it was time to test the lights – something both Alisha and Joanna would have done at the beginning!

The girls rushed to turn out the main light in the room to give the full effect when they turned the lights on, and a general hush was required. Simon and Joel made a big thing about counting them down from three then a big 'Tah-dah' and wouldn't you just believe it? The luck of a man – on came the fairy lights and everyone cheered.

The girls were eventually sent off to bed. After the four chatted for a while Simon made a move to go, too, saying if he didn't see them before they went for them both to have a fantastic holiday.

Joanna walked Simon to the door, and laid a hand on his arm, jokingly asking if he had the strength to drive home after such a busy day. He grasped hold of her hand and somehow she was against the wall in the passage. One of his arms was tightly wrapped around Joanna's body, drawing her close. The other hand brought her face to his and, as though he had waited all day long for this moment, his mouth descended on Joanna's. It moved and manipulated, kneaded and sucked, breathing hot breath into her very lungs.

The hand that had held up her chin had now strayed down to her breast, and his thumb was trailing lightly over her nipple. As Joanna gasped, the sensation running through her body was like molten liquid reaching deep down below the pit of her stomach to her womanly core, which she had almost forgotten existed. Simon lifted his lips slightly so that only a hair's breadth existed between them, and she thought she heard him whisper, "Soon, my darling, soon." But she would never be sure as she could hear nothing but the thumping of her own blood pressure pounding in her ears as her lungs drew in much needed air.

Simon kissed her one last time then drew his hands away purposefully, as though reprimanding himself for allowing himself to lose control. He leaned his forehead against Joanna's and, as they both opened their eyes, he said in a honey-smooth voice, "I have to go away for one last trip, but I'll be back for 'our' Christmas."

Joanna's heart flopped down to her boots on hearing that he was going away again. She knew without a shadow of a doubt that her heart would perish without him now and forever, she thought.

"This is my very last trip, but, I'm afraid, it's a very important one. If it all goes according to plan I'll tell you all about it when I get back."

Joanna was still mulling over the 'our Christmas' and she nodded her agreement, saying she understood and not to worry about her.

"Oh, but I do."

With one gentle squeeze on Joanna's arms he left. With a flash of his lights, Simon was gone, into the darkness, leaving Joanna to sort all these new feelings and insinuations out on her own.

Chapter 25

Excitement ensued as suitcases began to fill gradually with holiday clothes and gifts that Alisha and Joel were taking to give out. Joel kept telling Alisha that she couldn't take the kitchen sink and that they would never get her case through Customs. The bathroom scales were permanently moving from one bedroom to another so that they could weigh each case.

Joanna gave Alisha and Joel their Christmas presents she had bought them to open once they got to their sunny destination as it would make more sense. She had bought Joel a pair of knee-length shorts with huge flowers as she knew he would love them. For Alisha she had bought a beautiful sarong as she kept saying she was fat and wouldn't want to be seen in a bathing costume. And for Precious she had bought a lovely tankini and a pair of flip-flops.

It was as they gave their presents that it suddenly dawned on them that they wouldn't all be together for Christmas for the first time in five years.

Joanna and Alisha hugged each other tearfully and Joel made light of them, saying, "I will be lying in the sun on a beautiful beach with the blue sea lapping at my toes, instead of freezing my toes off in this country kicking my old car to get it moving in the snow."

But, as he came to hug Joanna, his squeeze was just a little bit tighter. He said, "If there is anything you need, you ring us. You have the number, don't you?"

Alisha was laughing, asking, "Who's worrying now? Joanna will cope better than we will without her to organise us. And, besides, she will have Simon." This was said with an outrageous Caribbean drawl, then they both said together, "Yeah, man."

The week flew by all too soon. Then the suitcases were being loaded into Joel's old car and they were all hugging each other saying to have a wonderful time and that they hoped they hadn't forgotten anything. At last, they were away in a flurry of slamming car doors and frantic waving. Their plane wouldn't be leaving for a couple of hours but they had to be at the airport for six a.m., which had been a mad struggle but they would make it.

Holly and Joanna closed the door once they had driven away. Joanna tried not to feel sad. I won't mope, she thought. It's Christmas, and I have a lot to do.

The first thing was to get to work. Holly and Joanna had two more days of post to deliver before the Christmas holiday. Joanna had asked for Christmas Eve off so that she could spend the day with Holly. She knew that Holly would miss Precious on that day as normally they would be driving each other mad trying to guess what they were getting for Christmas and it would be very strange for Holly this year.

As they pulled into the old station drive, Joanna couldn't help hoping to see a car parked there. However, there was no sign, to which Holly said, "Oh, Simon isn't here, unless his car is round the back, do you think, Mummy?"

"I wouldn't build your hopes up, darling. He did say he would be away on business, but he won't be away much longer."

"He won't miss Christmas, Mummy, will he? He will be home by then, won't he?"

"Darling, he will be home if he possibly can, but he has a very important job…" Her voice trailed away as Holly dashed out of the van to see Lily and William, and their Christmas tree, which she could see in the window right next to where William had watched for her coming.

William's face was a picture. He had not only recognised the little red van but his eyes lit up when he saw Holly. She went straight over to William and kissed him on the cheek and hugged him round the neck, which she had taken to doing as she almost thought of him as a grandfather now. He gripped her little hand and smiled warmly. No one would ever have suspected that this was the same person who, only three months ago, had had a face as blank as a blackboard and seemed to be without coherent thought.

They sat and had their coffee. Lily said that she had expected Simon would have returned by now; however, he had rung to say that he would be home 'now that everything was dealt with'. "Whatever that means," she mused.

Joanna and Lily puzzled for a moment, until their attention shifted to Holly, who was pointing out the little decorations on the Christmas tree in the window to William. She patiently went through each one, telling William carefully what they were, as well as a catalogue of the decorations they had on their Christmas tree at home. William looked as though he understood every word, and, what's more, he looked interested in every little thing Holly said.

"When I see Holly and William together, I feel as though I can see a fleeting glimpse of how William would have been with his own grandchildren. You'll never know how grateful we are to you and Holly and all your friends. Do you know, I think it was the luckiest day the day I broke my ankle and the roofers came to my door. Otherwise, I would never have had the pleasure of all your company, and help from each and every one of you." Lily leaned over to Joanna and squeezed her arm in a gesture of unspoken friendship.

They talked a little more about how they were looking forward to spending Christmas Day with them. Naturally, Joanna warned Lily about preparing too much, saying also that she would help her, so for her not to tire herself out cooking for five people. She had enough to do looking after William. Lily shushed Joanna, saying that it would be an absolute pleasure.

"You know, I used to prepare dinner parties for nine and ten people years ago, when William brought business colleagues home. I thought nothing of it then, and in some ways I miss those days."

"Yes, I know you do, but, Lily, you were a lot younger then, and fitter, and you didn't have a full-time job looking after William."

"That's the trouble, Joanna. I love William and I don't regret a moment of looking after him, but… Sometimes I really wish that I could be really useful again. Just to do something that wasn't simply homecare, do you know what I mean? Oh, don't listen to me, I don't mean to moan, but sometimes I feel I'm too young to be classed as an 'old person'. They say when doctors and policeman look young to you then that's the sign of old age, but surely that doesn't mean it's the end, does it?"

"No, no, Lily, you have a mind as sharp as Miss Marple's. Remember when you were going to brain Simon with the rolling pin? You caught on fast that night. No, I'm positive, when you are moved and Simon is with you, you will be able to help in some way. William is improving and I'm sure he will progress a lot more now that he has started."

"Yes, but he will miss you all so much. He will especially miss Holly. I genuinely think he gets excited when he sees her... Oh, listen to me. Stop me, for goodness sake, wittering on."

Joanna could see that Lily never wanted to complain as she was a naturally kind and caring person, but she could also see her mind wasn't being stretched. Joanna knew exactly how she was feeling, but she had no answers for her, or herself, come to that.

Tuesday and Wednesday were mad panic days; the last two days at work were frantic. She intended to spend Christmas Eve completely with Holly – they were going to 'chillax', as Holly told her Joel had said was the new word. Joanna assumed that it meant lazing about, which was exactly what she was going to do. But first they would have to tackle the heaving supermarket where they gave food away, or so it would seem by the size of the queues.

Holly had actually enjoyed the last two days of Joanna's run, as lots of Joanna's customers had got to know Holly and had brought little gifts to her for Christmas as they did for Joanna every year. They knew that Joanna delivered the mail no matter what, she lugged great big parcels that really should have arrived by parcel post, but she never complained. And, no matter what the weather was like, she never moaned and they were grateful for it.

Joanna thought that some of her customers must think she was an alcoholic, as the box she put her little presents in clinked with all the bottles of 'booze' that she would never get through in a year. She did like the odd glass of wine, but that was all. Still, it was all gladly accepted and would stock the drinks cupboard for Joel.

Christmas Eve arrived and still Joanna hadn't heard a word from Simon. She thought she would ring Lily later to see if everything was all right, then felt perhaps she shouldn't in case it might worry her. Joanna decided that nothing was going to stop her and Holly spending quality time together for the first time in her grown-up life.

As a real treat they lay on the sofa still in their nightwear watching a Walt Disney tear-jerker until after ten o'clock in the morning. A real Christmas snow, and bells that you couldn't help shedding a tear at even though you'd seen the film a million times before. Then Holly suggested they make mince pies to take to William and Lily's on Christmas Day. The house smelled wonderful and Joanna had just popped a casserole in the oven as a quick meal for herself and Holly when the doorbell flashed.

As Joanna went to the front door, her heart lurched. She could see a tall figure through the pebble glass and, hoping it wasn't her postman delivering a parcel, she pulled open the door.

To her absolute joy, it was Simon, whom she couldn't see immediately as he was hidden behind a huge bouquet of red roses. As he put the flowers to one side to see her face, his lips found hers, and he said, "Merry Christmas, Joanna."

A huge voice from behind shouted, "Simon," and Holly came running to greet him with a massive hug. Simon picked her up and swung her round as though she was as light as a feather.

"We didn't think you were going to make it. Mummy and Lily were really worried about you, but I knew you wouldn't not come at Christmas. But you nearly missed Santa Clause – if you had been any later. He comes tonight, you know?"

"No way! Not tonight, is it? I haven't bought any presents yet," Simon said, feigning distress at the thought of not having any presents.

"Oh, don't worry. Mummy and I have presents for you so you will have some to open, but Santa might have more for you. He always has for me. Well, as long as I behave, he has."

She cast a questioning look at Joanna, and Joanna smiled, saying she was sure that Holly had been good enough and she thought Santa would bring her some surprises.

Holly chattered away as she and Simon sat at the kitchen table. Joanna started to serve dinner for all three of them, assuming Simon would eat with them as he usually did. All the time Simon was talking to Holly, Joanna could feel the burn of his eyes on her back. They all sat down and enjoyed dinner, though it was a little strange with only three people. It was nice, actually. They chatted comfortably, and Holly watched as Joanna and Simon talked. It was as though she didn't want to intrude for fear of being in the way. Joanna had noticed that Holly hoped Simon would be a regular visitor to their house. To Holly, it must have felt a bit like having a daddy of her very own, just like Precious had.

After they had washed the dishes and Holly had shouted down that she was ready for bed, Joanna laughed, saying she wished that Holly would go to bed as early as this on normal nights. Chance would be a fine thing when Precious and Holly got together. They gossiped and giggled, and it was almost impossible to watch television in the lounge, the noise was so bad.

Just then an elephant came running down the stairs in the form of Holly. "I forgot! We haven't hung my stocking on the mantelpiece. Oh, normally Precious hangs hers there and mine goes under the clock."

Simon and Joanna looked at the excited little face with her beautiful, blond, wavy hair and eyes so bright. All newly bathed and hair washed, she could have passed for an angel. The stocking once done, she was eventually ready for Santa Clause to arrive. She went over to Simon, put her arms around his neck and kissed him on the cheek, saying in a tear-jerking way that would melt any heart, "Merry Christmas, Simon. I'm glad you're here."

Simon was visibly shaken as he gave Holly a kiss on her cheek, saying, "Merry Christmas, Holly. I'm very happy to be here. Sleep tight."

Chapter 26

Simon was seated on the sofa and had turned out the main lights, leaving only the flicker of the gas-fired flames in the hearth and the coloured fairy lights on the Christmas tree in the corner of the room when Joanna came downstairs after settling Holly.

It was obvious to Joanna that Holly's words had visibly moved him. Holly had that way about her – she had an ethereal quality that was almost angelic at times.

Simon patted the seat next to his so that Joanna couldn't mistake his meaning and sit opposite in a chair. She sat down a little shyly, until Simon put his arm firmly around her shoulders, and she began to relax into it. He started by saying he had a lot to tell her. But he hadn't been able to say anything until it had been seen and proved.

Joanna wasn't sure what he was saying, but she assumed it had something to do with the new business. However, she was wrong.

"Do you remember when we came home from Scotland and Lydia was there?"

"Yes, and she had hardly any clothes on," Joanna said bravely.

"Yes," said Simon in an amusing way, "and we all nearly died of embarrassment, especially me."

"You? Why would you be embarrassed? It was your mum and me who didn't know where to look."

Simon said he felt embarrassed just thinking about it, how she had draped herself all over him in front of Joanna and his mother of all people.

Joanna laughed at that – a man of Simon's age and experience being embarrassed in front of his mum.

"Now behave. I'm trying my hardest, here, to explain about a very tricky situation, so hush."

Joanna swallowed any retort she was about to say and did just that.

"Well, to cut a long story short, when Lydia produced my driving licence I knew there was something fishy because my licence is kept in my wallet. It could not have fallen out on to 'our' bedroom floor. Hush, hush, I'm coming to that. I always put my wallet and spare money on the dressing table of the room in the flat where the whole crew share," Simon explained.

"It's pointless all of us having separate flats or hotel rooms when we only stay over for maybe one night or two, and hardly ever together. We all know each other and so it makes perfect sense to share one flat with three bedrooms. But we do not share a bedroom. Whoever uses the flat takes a bedroom – we don't share beds."

Joanna's face visibly relaxed and Simon took his queue to carry on. "So the little scene that she carried out in front of you and my mother was silly and careless of her. To be honest, that in itself rang alarm bells. After all, why should she turn up at my home, which by the way she got the address for from my licence? Especially dressed like that."

"Or undressed." Joanna couldn't help but chirp in, and Simon gave her a playful squeeze.

"Well, her general manner was altogether strange. She was overly familiar – something she had never been. There has never been anything more than a casual drink between us. She did know that I wanted to set up my own company. But what she hadn't realised was that I had taken a month's leave suddenly. If you remember, it was because I was worried about Mum.

"Well, that must have caused her real problems, as she had been smuggling small shipments of drugs in and the captain must sign the import sheets. When you work with someone for a long time you, rightly or wrongly, trust them. Well, of course, she must have needed my signature and at some point she must have stolen my licence. I, of course, never noticed. I only ever use it when I come home to hire a car. So she had to make that elaborate story up to explain her visit."

"She was not going to be your partner in the business then?"

"No way, definitely not. Lydia isn't a pilot, she is a stewardess. This is my business – the whole reason of branching out on my own is that I can do what I want. Anyway, it all clicked into place when Gatwick called me and told me that certain packages had been signed for with my name and signature. However, a sharp-eyed baggage handler had queried the signature."

"Don't tell me Alisha was right after all… Drugs?"

"Clever Alisha, and, of course, as I had made the hasty decision to leave almost immediately, Lydia had to find a way of convincing her supplier that she could not only pay off what she owed him, but that she could also deliver more on a regular basis."

"Alisha said, when people behave strangely and have ups and downs like Lydia appeared to have, there are usually drugs involved. When the children saw her in a very angry conversation they said she was really scary."

"Lydia made the fatal mistake of not noticing the girls. And also assuming that they wouldn't know what she was talking about. I had mentioned that they were both deaf to her earlier. The girls, as you know, innocently thought Lydia was talking about transporting handbags and not bags of drugs."

"Oh my God, Simon, it's like something you see on the television and not real life."

"Anyway, that's why I had to do one last flight. It was being monitored by Customs and Excise, and 'bingo', she was careless. She must have made copies of my signature to use when she needed, and her need became more desperate so she took chances.

"She even thought, in some fantasy dream of hers, that she was going to come to Scotland. And that we would live together and she would carry on smuggling in my planes. She had even, in her fantasy, decided Mum and Dad would go and live in a home. I hadn't actually realised how 'out of it' she had become.

"I was taken back when she arrived in that manner but it still didn't click that she was hooked on drugs. But by the following day, when she said she had to find a chemist so desperately, I was beginning to wonder what on earth was wrong with her."

"You mean you are used to half-naked women draping themselves all over you so that wasn't so unusual," said Joanna in a provocative manner, knowing Simon would react, which he did. He turned her face towards his and, as he did, he pulled her down so they were lying comfortably against the arm of the sofa. He took hold of one of Joanna's arms, putting it above her head, while the other hand traced the pattern on her sweater. What had started as innocent fun soon changed, as the sexual tension that had been bottled up inside both of them became apparent.

Simon deviated his hand to the hem of Joanna's sweater as his lips pressed hard and demanding against hers. His fingers reached her swollen breast and Joanna gasped in anticipation. Simon expertly released Joanna's bra, and the heat they generated between them could have warmed a house. As Simon's fingers caressed Joanna's waiting breasts and Joanna's gasps became small whimpers, Simon seemed to pull his senses together, asking Joanna, "Are you sure, Joanna? Are you absolutely sure? We can stop now, but, oh, Joanna, I really want to make love to you."

Joanna could hardly think, but one thing she did know. Whatever happened, whatever the future had in store, she wanted to make love to Simon. She wanted this one night if nothing else. For her answer she pulled his head down to her mouth, saying, "Yes, Simon, yes, it's what I want."

Simon rose up from the warmth of the comfortable sofa that held such temptation for them to stay. But they both knew the last thing they would ever want was for Holly to come down and see them. Simon carried Joanna upstairs and she gently pushed the bedroom door open. The bedside lamp gave off a warm glow, and as they sank on to the soft duvet their kisses deepened. They began to pull each other's clothes off in earnest. The tension between them grew to fever pitch, and Joanna couldn't believe her ears when Simon's throaty, passion-filled voice said in a mixture of a groan and a sigh, "I love you, Joanna. I've loved you almost since the very beginning."

That was all Joanna needed to know. This time, she thought to herself, this time I get to keep this family. This one's mine.

She whispered back in her tortured, tear-filled voice, "And, oh, how I love you, Simon."

Their lovemaking was frantic, fast and passionate, with a tumultuous release. Then no sooner had their breathing returned to normal than a single touch of the hand made their senses strain to be released once again.

They lay wrapped in each other's arms, exhausted, satiated and contented. They kissed, simply revelling in their closeness.

Joanna looked at the clock. "I hate to tell you this, but there is one thing about having children and trying to have…"

"A sex life," Simon finished for her as Joanna was still a little embarrassed to talk openly with him yet.

"Yes, one of those, but Santa Clause is coming tonight. And I have got to lay Holly's presents under the tree or she'll think she must have been a very bad girl indeed. I'm sorry, but that's what being a parent is all about, I'm afraid," Joanna said in an apologetic way.

Simon turned her towards him, kissing her gently but firmly, saying, "But, my darling, that's exactly what I want. I want to be part of this family, if you and Holly will let me, and if need be I'll climb down the chimney as Santa Clause."

"Ha ha, you would have a hard time, we are all gas. Seriously though, do you really Simon? Do you really want to be part of our family?" This was said with the biggest lump in Joanna's throat.

She was afraid even to breathe until he replied, "I do, I really do, if you'll let me. I have never been happier than I am when I am with you and Holly."

"Do you know how long I've waited for someone to say that to me? You can never know how much it means to me, never, but one day I'll tell you. For now, you had better get your handsome body out of my bed and ready to start hauling presents out of the wardrobe where they are hidden and downstairs before Holly wakes up."

Joanna slipped on her winter red, velvet bathrobe and, after finding one of Joel's from their bedroom, she gave Simon the wonderfully flamboyant striped robe that suited Joel perfectly and that Simon also looked good enough to eat in. Then again, thought Joanna, on reflection he would look good in a bin bag.

After they had laid all the presents under the tree, Simon poured each of them a glass of wine and tapped the sofa. They resumed their comfortable position in front of the warm fire, relaxed in each other's arms. Simon reached into his pocket and brought out a small package. Turning to Joanna, he told her it was for her to open now.

"What, before Santa Clause has even been?"

As Joanna opened the little package her heart was pounding. Part of her knew it was a jewellery box, but she never believed anything until it happened. She had learned that lesson when she was a child.

With the wrapping disposed of, she held her breath before opening the box to see, sparkling up at her, the most gorgeous deep blue sapphire. It was shaped like a lozenge and surrounded by tiny diamonds mounted on gold.

The lessons learned from childhood were hard to forget, so Joanna didn't attempt to put the ring on her finger for fear of placing it on the wrong one. Simon looked at her face in order to gauge if she was happy, but all he could see was uncertainty.

"Will you marry me, Joanna? Will you come to Scotland and start a new adventure with us?"

A huge breath exhaled from Joanna's lungs, and, after taking another deep breath and making a silent prayer, she said, with eyes full of tears of relief, "Oh yes, Simon, yes, I would love to marry you and start a new adventure."

The End

Epilogue

Their wedding was very low key. Their imminent move had been put on temporary hold, which allowed every one who was important to be with Joanna, Simon and Holly for their special day. Holly and Precious got to be flower girls, even though it was a simple registry office wedding. The girls looked delightful in their long dresses of rich red velvet; and they carried tiny little posies of holly, covered in bright red berries mixed with miniature white carnations.

A small reception after the ceremony, consisting of both families, was held in a private room in a country hotel. Many tears of joy were shed by everyone except Simon, who was like the cat that had drunk the cream.

Joel and Alisha talked of their relief as they had not known how they were going to explain to Joanna that Joel had been offered a consultant's post in one of Bridgetown's most respected hospitals, which he really would like to accept. The icing on the cake was that a bungalow by the sea was part of the deal.

And most surprising of all was that Alisha was pregnant, which she was sure had happened on their romantic holiday in Bermuda. They laughed and said it was all Simon's fault, but that they would always be grateful to him.

Precious was thrilled at the thought of having a sibling, although she was sad that Holly, whom she thought of as a sister, would not be with her. Assured of future holidays, where they would see each other again, the girls were excited about all the new things they were about to experience.

It was obvious to Joanna, on their return, that Joel and Alisha had known Simon's intentions all the time. That's why they hadn't worried about leaving her over Christmas. Simon had quite obviously informed them of his future plans.

The move to Scotland was almost seamless. Simon had sent a team of builders and decorators into the house. And between Lily and Joanna it was obvious that settling into their new home was not going to be a problem.

Lily appeared to have shed ten years since William's improvement continued. She even began to help organise the office paperwork for the newly formed Cargo & Courier Service. Holly and William were like best friends. His continual improvement astounded each of the consultants. He was naturally never expected to return to his old self; however, the change in his ability meant that Lily was able to take a much more active role in the business, and spend less time on his domestic care.

Simon insisted, when organising the office arrangements, that Joanna had a small office space of her very own. This, he said, was for her to set up her own Personal Advocacy Service. He wanted Joanna to realise her dream as he had his. One of Joanna's first jobs, while becoming a general thorn in the side of anyone who caused upset to those who could not speak for themselves, was a documented file of two cases of fraud. She had the names and addresses of the companies involved, which she sent to a television programme that dealt with 'rogue traders'. The feeling of satisfaction it gave her when the programme took up her case studies of the rogue roofers and builders made Joanna more determined than ever to make sure there would always be somewhere for those who need help to find it.

There was great excitement on the morning on which Simon was to bring the first plane home. When he radioed that he was about to land, they all stood outside the office and watched this auspicious occasion. As he landed and flashed his lights, Simon took out of the cargo bay of the plane a crate. He carried it over to the waiting group, all wrapped up against the bitter cold.

Then he opened the wire crate so that they could clearly see what it contained – the most gorgeous golden Labrador dog. Holly bent down to comfort it as it was released from the cage. This was a moment that Holly would never forget. As Simon introduced them to each other, Simon told Holly that she was a very special dog. She was specially trained to be her ears. She would go everywhere with her, even to the village school that Holly was to attend.

Holly gave Simon almost as big a hug as she did her new best friend, which he announced would be called 'Precious'.